EVERWORLD

FEAR THE FANTASTIC

K. A. APPLEGATE

SCHOLASTIC INC.
New York Toronto London Auckland Sydney
Mexico City New Delhi Hong Kong

For Michael

and Jake

ISBN 0-590-87764-X

12 11 10 9 8 7 6 5 4 3 3 4 5 6/0

Printed in the U.S.A.

First Scholastic printing, March 2000

Chapter I

So, basically, things were looking pretty good.

We had escaped from Fairy Land — which was not as easy as it sounds. We had avoided being incinerated by Nidhoggr, the dragon the size of Rhode Island, who guards the back door to Hel's Happy Underground Party World. We had sold our half-a-satyr at a profit — we paid nothing for him to begin with. We'd created the first-ever communications corporation, becoming the AT&T of Fairy Land, and we'd been paid off in a couple of big handfuls of diamonds.

We were rich, carefree, happy-go-lucky teenagers.

And gee golly gosh, life would have been just swell, just keen, just peachy, except there were a whole bunch of folks after us: Loki, Norse god of insane offspring; Hel, his half-dead, half-babe daughter; his middle child, the Midgard Serpent (who makes Nidhoggr look like a tadpole); Fenrir, Loki's wolf son who's big enough to crap a sofa; and Merlin, who isn't Loki's kid and probably isn't evil but can nevertheless make dead sheep jump up and bite your throat out.

And now, as my sleep-crusted eyelids fluttered open, and I was yanked unwillingly back across from the real world — where I was convincing a girl in a chat room that I was a twenty-five-year-old software billionaire — I realized there was one other small matter, one other small complaint, one other tiny cloud to darken my normally sunny worldview: We had wandered into Hetwan country.

I raised this matter calmly with David.

"Look! Oh, my God! Look up there. Oh, man. Oh, man. You know what those are? Those are freaking Hetwan. They're flying, man, there must be hundreds of them."

David shook his head. "More like thousands. Jalil and I have been watching them for a while."

"Excuse me? You and Jalil have been watching them? And yet we're not running like the scared rabbits we are?"

The two of them were standing there in the dark. Calmly looking up at the sky. David striking a heroic pose, head back, hands on hips, defiant, unimpressed, unafraid — or putting on a good act at least. The jackass.

And Jalil, observant, contemplative, a frown of deep thought on his smug, I'm-just-so-darned-smart face, arms folded across his chest.

April was still asleep, using her backpack as a pillow, scrunched on her side and looking like she needed someone to come and offer her some body warmth.

It was a thought. But this was not really the right time.

"Which way you going to run, Christopher?" David jerked his chin back in the direction we'd come. "Fairy Land's back that way. I don't think we're real popular back there. We are 'friends and known associates' of Nidhoggr. We go back that way, the little leprechauns are going to nail about four hundred arrows into us in the time between when we say, 'Don't,' and when we say, 'Shoot.'"

He was right about that. The fairies are fast. And not nearly as cute as they are in fairy tales. These fairies were businessmen and we'd cost them a chance to walk away with Nidhoggr's treasure.

I looked up at the moonlit sky. Up through the dark tree branches. Up to vulture altitude, up to where the Hetwan flew silently by in neat, well-ordered rows, like obedient third-graders on their way to the lunchroom.

They're aliens, the Hetwan. Thin, wispy, about Calista Flockhart size. Maybe a Calista and a quarter. They have bug eyes and insect mouth parts made of three little arm things that never stop grabbing at whatever insect or imagined insect might be flying by. And they have wings.

They're creepy, disturbing things. Then again, "creepy" and "disturbing" were the two most frequently used words at the local computer dating service. Everyone around here was creepy and disturbing.

The real problem with the Hetwan is that they serve some kind of boss god, some kind of Capo di Tutti Immortals, some kind of Bill Gates of gods, who eats other gods and spits out their god bones. He's called Ka Anor. He's bad. How bad? Bad enough that really bad, really violent, really hard, nasty, evil guys are scared of him.

Imagine Jeffrey Dahmer thinking someone else was really a hard-core psycho. "Hey, man, sure I kill guys and cut them up and put them in the freezer and cook certain body parts for lunch, but see that guy over there? That guy is *crazy!*"

Loki thinks Ka Anor is scary. Huitzilopoctli thinks Ka Anor is scary. And Huitzilopoctli eats fresh human hearts.

"Can they see us?" I asked, feeling the sudden, urgent need to pee. Preferably in a toilet far, far away.

David shrugged. "I don't know. Probably not. We don't have a fire going and they're pretty high up."

"They may have quite different visual receptors," Jalil suggested. "They may be attuned to movement, or see only in the infrared or ultraviolet range."

"Hey, I know, Jalil: Why don't you stand there and stare at them a while, then write a paper about them for extra credit? 'Stuff I noticed about the Ally McBugs before they ate my face.' What's the matter with you two?"

Jalil did his lizard-eye thing where he looks at you without moving his head. "Would it make you feel better if I was hysterical?"

"Yeah. Yeah, it would," I said. "I'd be very reassured if you would run around in circles tearing your hair out. At least that would make sense. What are we going to do?"

David shrugged. "I guess we should try and catch some z's. We start running around down here, we may just attract their attention. We're all exhausted. We need sleep. I'll take the first watch."

"Forget that, I'll take first watch," I said. "You

two are way too calm, trying to outmacho each other. I'll keep watch. I want some honest, human fear on duty."

I heard something stir. April.

"Whas happen?" she mumbled.

"Nothing. Go back to sleep. We got Hetwan flying over like B-29's on their way to bomb Berlin in some old war movie. No problem. Go back to sleep. I'll wake you up if one of them starts to chew on your feet."

Evidently my sarcasm wasn't sharp enough to wake her up. She snorted a "going to sleep" snort.

"B-25's," Jalil said. "B-29's were mostly used against Japan."

David handed me his sword. The sword he'd taken from the dying Galahad. "You cool, man? You okay?"

"Why wouldn't I be?" I grated. I hate David's penetrating, manly stare. His John-Wayne-slash-Clint-Eastwood thing. "Hey, there's only a thousand or so of them. And here I have your handy hero sword. Shouldn't be any problem, David."

He grinned, his teeth a kind of dashboard-saint white in the moonlight. "W.T.E, Christopher."

"Yeah. W.T.E."

W.T.E.: Welcome To Everworld.

Everworld.

A different universe. Literally.

When I was little we went to Disney World. I barfed on the submarine ride, after which I think they had to just sink the sub, because I blew chunks everywhere. Anyway, at Disney World my folks bought me a balloon. It was this double balloon. There's a Mickey-Mouse-shaped balloon inside of a translucent outer balloon. The Mickey ears never touched the outer balloon.

That's Everworld. A universe within or beside or next door to the real universe. Totally different rules. Definitely Mickey Mouse.

The story is that the old gods — Zeus and Odin and Quetzalcoatl and the Daghdha and Baal, and Jim Morrison, Hendrix, and Elvis for all I know, and the various other motley, malignant, insane, delusional Looney Tunes and immortal riffraff who were wandering around avoiding the Big Cosmic Rubber Room — all got together one fine day and said, "Hey, this place sucks, let's move."

So they created a new and different universe. One that operated according to their rules. They dragged enough trolls, elves, dwarfs, goblins, satyrs, nymphs, and humans along to provide a continuing source of entertainment. After all, what's the point in being Hel if you don't have anyone to torture? And what's Huitzilopoctli going to eat if there isn't a ready supply of still-pumping human hearts? Crackers?

The thing with gods is, they need an audience.

So, in any case, they created Everworld. And everything was fine till some outsiders stumbled into this private asylum. Other gods. Other immortals. But not from Earth.

And these gods drag their own assortment of yes-men, toadies, and freaks along. Because even if you're an alien immortal you need someone to quiver in fear every time you twitch.

Even then, I guess, it was fine. The old Earth gods got along with the new alien gods. Until Ka Anor showed up. He ate gods. Which caused some concern. It's one thing to mess with the common folk. But Ka Anor was shish-kebabbing the shish-kebabbers.

So Loki got the bright idea of moving back to the old neighborhood. He got his son Fenrir, with an assist from unnamed powers, to poke through the barrier between universes and snatch a person who could be used to form a permanent bridge between universes.

Then Loki, and whoever else wanted to bail out, could bail, move back to the real world, set up shop, design some cool Web sites, get themselves cable-access shows, recruit a few hundred thousand wack jobs, and go into the crazy cult business.

Then they could close the gate behind them, trap Ka Anor back in Everworld, and get down to the serious business of screwing up our already screwed-up world.

Swell plan. And the timing couldn't be better. If everything had worked out, Loki and Huitzilopoctli and Hel and the entire parade could have emerged into the Chicago area in time for Y2K.

But Loki lost his "witch," his gateway.

Her name is Senna Wales. I used to go with her. A strange, gray-eyed, wispy chick with impressive hardware and seriously corrupted software.

We'd already broken up by the time Fenrir

snatched her off a Lake Michigan pier. She was going with David by that point. And me, and David, and Jalil, and April all happened to be there watching when the first-ever intergalactic kidnapping took place.

We were dragged across the barrier, too. Or partly. Somehow we ended up in both places at once. There was a real-world Christopher. And an Everworld Christopher. Whenever Everworld me went to sleep I sort of snapped back into the continuing saga of boring, real-world me.

A great life. I could be dragon food one minute, fall asleep, and still have to face the SAT's.

Here's a news flash: Life isn't fair.

A fact that occurred to me yet again as I sat there on my bony butt, clutching a dead hero's sword and lifting my eyes to a huge moon illuminating alien silhouettes.

After a while the parade of Hetwan ended. I was relieved at that.

It occurred to me that we'd probably caused this exodus of Hetwan from Fairy Land and beyond. They'd been poised to invade the Underworld but they needed Nidhoggr out of the way and we'd ended up saving that blue whale of a dragon.

I considered waking up the others to tell them the air show was over. But that wouldn't have accomplished anything and, in any case, I was awake now. I had that buzzy, blurry, too-much-coffee-and-not-enough-sleep feeling. Like a day where you stayed out late the night before, possibly enjoying a few brews, then wake up too early from the alcohol metabolizing.

Anyway, I was awake. And the sky was losing

its black shine and becoming gray around the horizon. Once it was light we would be on the move again. Too little sleep. Too few showers. Too little food. Too many psychos. Way too much running and screaming. That summarized the Everworld experience.

I opened one of the gunnysacks of food we'd carried from Fairy Land, took out a small loaf of bread, and ripped off a chunk. It was good bread. Sweet-smelling from the herbs. Suddenly I was starving and I just lit into it, wolfing down most of the loaf.

Back home I'd be having eggs. No one in my house is a big health food nut. We eat eggs. Fried. Over medium, not too runny. Or scrambled, maybe with some fried salami or bacon or ham. Juice. Milk. Coffee.

The far horizon was phasing from gray to pink. Any minute now the sun would peek up over the rim of the world. Or maybe it was some god dragging a big light across the sky, who knew? Maybe the world was still round here, and the sun was still the sun. Or maybe not.

"I would sell my mother for a glass of milk," I muttered. "Two percent, whole milk, even one percent. Anything but skim as long as it is ice-cold. Bye, Mom, but I need my milk. I'm a growing boy."

The sun edged up. And then a howling, a keening, a wailing.

I jumped to my feet. David jerked up. April spun, stumbled to her feet, and brushed the tumbled haystack of auburn hair out of her face. Jalil sat up.

"What is that?" David asked me.

I shook my head. The sound was growing, swelling, seeming to roll across the face of the earth, a far-off choir that was galloping toward us.

All on our feet. All very, very awake. David took his sword back.

The sound was still swelling, not so much from volume as from new "voices" being added. Like a hundred people were singing at one level, and another fifty joined in, and another fifty, and more and more.

And as it grew, the sound changed subtly. You didn't so much think "moaning" as "singing." Like a psalm in church: a little mournful, a little shaky, but gaining confidence as it approached some well-remembered chorus.

The sun, golden fire, suddenly burned on the horizon, and the sound, the voices, the choir, whatever it was let out a gasp of joy.

"Ah!" April cried, almost joining in unconsciously.

Pink and pale blue and orange streaked the gray sky, and the sound, the sound was becoming emotional. It wasn't threatening, it wasn't dangerous-sounding, but it was huge and everywhere without being loud. I was a bug walking across a woofer and fearing that someone was going to crank the volume up to ten. It was all around me, everywhere the sun's rays reached, everywhere that the shadows gave way was filled with The Sound.

And now I could see well enough to become very, very nervous. We were in the middle of a landscape that looked like what you'd get if Salvador Dalí and Dr. Seuss had worked together.

It was flat, basically. Flat as Kansas. Except that someone had come along with a gigantic ice-cream scoop and hollowed out deep, plunging, almost perfectly round valleys. Then the ice cream had been piled up here and there in improbable rounded hills one, two, three scoops high.

We were within twenty feet of the edge of one of the big holes. We hadn't even known it. The bush where I'd gone to do my business in the night was maybe one body-length away from a sheer drop.

But as weird as this basic geography was, it was what covered the hills and the land and filled the valleys that made it clear we were a very, very long way from Old Orchard Mall.

They were trees. Like palm trees in that they had long, serpentine trunks. Like maples or elms or oaks in that at the top they suddenly sprouted robust branches. The leaves ranged from pointy, French-cooking-knife shapes to fans to six-pointed stars to large, flat pie plates with cutouts in the shape of triangles or eye slits.

The leaves were sea-foam green and pink and burnt orange and rain-slicker yellow. And some were mirrors that caught the sun's strengthening rays and seemed almost to catch fire, so that as I looked down into the neatly circular valley or back at the triple-scoop mountain or at the trees swaying over my head, I was dazzled and blinded by glittering, reflected light.

It was the trees that were making the sound. As the light neared they moaned in anticipation. As they lit up, they cried out in wordless joy. Then, as the sun blazed off their mirrors and through their cutouts, the trees mellowed into a satisfied hum.

And all of this seemed to extend forever before us and around us. The only zone of silence and relative calm was back in the direction from which we'd come.

"It's beautiful," April said, her tone neatly balanced between delight and incredulity.

"This is Hetwan country?" I wondered.

"Guess so," David said. "Not exactly what I was expecting."

"What were you expecting?" Jalil asked him.

"I don't know. Like a termite mound or an ant colony. I mean, they're insects. Aren't they?"

"They're aliens," Jalil answered. "I'm not sure if they're insects, really. They look like our concept of bugs. Aside from the fact that they walk erect."

"Really big bugs."

"It's beautiful," Jalil said. "It's amazing. Doesn't mean the creatures that live here are friendly."

"Yeah," I agreed.

"The jungle's pretty, too. Spiders, leopards, snakes."

I said, "You know, after the old Midgard Serpent, it's gonna take an awful lot of snake to impress me."

"So what do we do? Where do we go?" April asked. She yawned.

"The devil we know versus the devil we don't," David said. "Go back and the fairies get us for sure. Go forward, we don't know."

"The fairy queen said Ka Anor only eats gods," April pointed out.

"Hey, yeah!" I said. "That's right. She was a sharp old crone. She must know, right? Anyway, the Hetwan who was there didn't say anything different."

"The Hetwan aren't talkative," Jalil said. "But I think you guys are probably right. I think the fairy queen knew what she was talking about. The fairies weren't acting like the Hetwan were nothing, but they weren't falling to their knees every time Ka Anor's name came up."

We were talking ourselves into walking deeper into Hetwan country. It was the singing and the landscape. It was affecting us, lulling us, dulling the Gillette edge of my usual fear. I knew all this. But it really was hard to see anything terrible happening in a place where the trees sing.

"Ka Anor is the root of the whole problem," April said. "Ka Anor has destabilized things. He is the Everworld revolution. If he were gone . . ."

This snapped me out of my dreamy "isn't it all just ever so lovely?" state of mind.

"Don't even start down that road again, April," I warned. "Our mission, should we decide to accept it — and of course we don't have a choice — is to stay alive and haul our pansy asses back to the land of seat belts, multivitamins, and looking both ways before you cross the street. I'm thinking that us all going off to kill some schizo alien god-eater who's surrounded by an army of thousands of flying bug-monkeys is not the best way to retain the aforementioned pansy ass."

Jalil cocked an eyebrow. "I didn't know you knew the word 'aforementioned.' Let alone that you could use it in a sentence."

"Even crackers take business English," I shot back. "What, so you're okay with this, Jalil? Us going off to solve all the problems of Everworld armed with a sword and your two-inch knife?"

He shook his head. "No. I'm not okay with it."

"Me neither," David admitted. "Basic military common sense: Four people do not decide to attack a force of tens of thousands. I'm thinking we keep moving, keep our heads down, try to find the shortest way out of all this, back into whatever piece of earth may be nearby. What's that noise?"

"The trees," April said. "Weird. They're sharp."

"Say what?"

Suddenly the volume of the trees rose, and sure enough, they were sharp. They were building up to out-and-out screeching, screaming, howling. But all from one direction. Like a wave of sonic misery rolling toward us.

I saw treetops toppling in the distance. Then, very suddenly, I saw the wood chippers.

Army ants. That was the first impression. Only these were way too big to be ants. These things were the size of ponies. And roughly a third of that size was devoted to a mouth about as big around as a manhole cover.

There were hundreds. Maybe thousands. A herd. A swarm. A wave, crashing through and swirling around the trees. Climbing over one another on their uncounted rat feet.

Three of them annihilated one of the pink mirror trees in thirty seconds. Chewed it up like beavers on crack. One chopped it down with a series of lightning-fast chomps, then, even as the tree fell, another would leap up and start gnawing on its midsection. The third would catch the treetop, the branches, and launch into the leaves.

I flashed for one hideous, frozen instant on the wood chipper scene from *Fargo*.

Then I ran.

I was not alone. The four of us tore back the way we'd come, back toward Fairy Land, each having the identical thought that if we had to die, a fairy arrow through the neck was a lot better than being chewed up and crapped out as sawdust.

The trees were screaming all around us now — how did trees scream, did they have mouths, too? *Run! Don't ask dumb questions, run!* Howling and shrieking all around us, the trees, they knew the monsters were coming this way, knew they were about to be pulped. Them and anything that got in the way.

"The pit!" David yelled.

The pits? He thought this was the pits? That was his comment? The pits? What was he, Richie Cunningham all of a sudden?

Oh, the pit! The hole, the valley. Yeah, yeah, run!

The edge of the drop was on my left. Just past April, who wasn't wasting any more time than I was. Two things are really scary: running away, and seeing someone else run away. You see someone else, their face all distorted by fear, eyes wide, cheeks red, mouth pulled back in a toothy, skeletal grin, well, that's not reassuring.

I heard David cry out. I shot a look toward the sound. I saw him go down like a skier who can't quite outrun the avalanche. He just toppled backward, arms flung out, mouth open, fell back and was gone.

Then the beavers were on us, a wall of teeth and sweaty fur and frenzied energy. They were a rolling lava spill of destruction, ripping, chewing, straining to find the next thing to destroy, and the next thing was me.

Twenty feet. So fast! Ten.

I cut left. Slammed into April. She said a word she saves for serious situations. We sprawled. I bounced up like a drop of water in a hot frying pan. Down-Up. A single movement, fall and rise. Like I was made of rubber.

Not fast enough, I could feel hot breath on me, teeth filling my field of vision. I screamed a girly scream and leaped.

Into nothingness.

April and I fell, screaming. About ten feet. Maybe more, maybe less, I wasn't reeling out the tape measure. I was screaming like the entire cast of *I Know What You Did Three Summers Ago*.

I hit. Heels first. Face into bushes. Rolled. Branches, leaves, dirt, dirt jamming into my mouth, fingers clawing, legs kicking, looking for a level surface.

Down and down. Stop. I was against a tree trunk. Looking . . . down? Up? My eyes had stopped working for me, they were on their own, refusing to focus. Then they snapped. Focus.

Focus on a wall of the wood chippers spilling off the cliff above me like lemmings. The tree I was leaning against — my back possibly broken, and my kidneys definitely bruised — started yowling. I could feel the tree's voice vibrating my spine.

I did Scooby-Doo legs, feet flying. My heel caught something, I spun on my side, on the dirt, spun, legs over head, rolled and tumbled away from the tree, which three seconds later was falling and being chomped in midair.

I tried to stand. The wave hit me. Giant beavers stuck on fast forward nailed me to the ground. I rolled onto my belly and they were all over me. A stampede. Hundreds of rat feet slapped me. I was blinded by the dirt thrown up all around me. Smothered by the sleek fur pressed close.

But no one was eating me.

Then, sudden release. They were past. They were past, and when I dug the dirt out of my eyes and nose and mouth I could look back up the scooped-out cliff face and see a swath cut right through the trees. Stumps. Not even stumps, what was left was too low to qualify as stumps.

And below me, and down, and across the floor of the valley, a neat swath of disappeared trees.

The herd was roaring up the far side of the valley now, with the trees all screaming.

I stood up. Shaky. Bruised. The taste of vomit in my mouth. Heart slamming blood through my arteries with so much pressure that a pinprick would have sent me flying and whipping like an uncontrolled fire hose.

"April?!" I yelled.

"Unh."

"What?"

"Down here."

I slid down the slope. Easy to do. A lot easier than going up. April was looking about like I probably looked. Like a few hundred alien tree-eating monsters had just run over her.

"You okay?" I asked. I gave her a hand getting up.

"Of course I'm okay," she spat. "Never better. Let's get back up there, out of here."

She tried to lead the way. But it was almost vertical. And the ground was freshly plowed, not so much as a stiff dirt clod to hold on to.

David and Jalil appeared at the top of this cliff.

"What are you guys doing down there?" David called down.

"What are we doing? We're inventing the new sport of dirt surfing."

"Pretty steep," David commented.

"Do you think so?" April snapped. "We hadn't noticed. Hey, Christopher, it's steep. That's our problem here: steepness. I am really filthy, I have dirt and sawdust in my underwear, so don't piss me off."

It was a ridiculous situation. David and Jalil and the relative normalcy of flat land were no more than twelve feet above my upstretched arms. But we could not make that last dozen feet. It was like trying to climb up a wall.

"Go over to the trees that are still standing," Jalil suggested. "You can brace yourself on them, maybe."

So April and I crab-walked horizontally to the edge of the path of devastation. Over to the softly humming, untouched trees. I wedged my foot against the base of one of these. Which accomplished nothing. None of the trees grew uphill from this one. I considered shinnying up, back against the tree, feet against the cliff, but the angles were all wrong.

I looked back toward the swath of destruction. Only the swath wasn't nearly as destroyed as it should be. "Hey. Those trees are growing back."

The trees were growing at a fantastic rate. Not

shooting up from the ground or anything, but growing fast enough that I could actually see movement. A little tendril with tiny leaves formed straight in the center of the stump. It grew and thickened. Maybe an inch every two minutes. And made a buzzing-bee sound as it grew.

"Half an inch a minute," April muttered. "What's that, thirty inches an hour? Two and a half feet?"

"What are you guys thinking of doing?" Jalil yelled down.

"I think we're thinking of grabbing onto one of these trees as it grows and letting it lift us up," I said. I looked at April. She looked like a raccoon. There were circles of more-or-less clean flesh around her eyes, and mud-pack everywhere else. "That is what we're thinking, right?"

That was what we were thinking.

It took a few hours, during which time we waited and talked and wandered around till the tree had grown a little over six feet. Then we wedged ourselves into the still-forming upper branches and waited. Waited.

And I, at least, fell asleep.

I was in town. Walking along Church Street, wearing suspiciously neat, clean clothing.

Oh, my God. I was job hunting.

It was evening. And this being early fall it was half-light still at six-thirty. The street lights were on, the car lights were mostly on, I could see into bright businesses full of bored drones and slightly less bored customers.

I received the CNN: Breaking News update from Everworld Christopher. Apparently he/I had been run over by a stampede of tree-chomping megarats.

And now the Everworld Christopher was sitting in a tree that was growing in a way that reminded me very much of watching the little blue bar at the bottom of my Web browser. I mean, I knew it was fast for a tree, but damn it was slow.

Here in the real world, I'd been trolling for work. Christmas was still a couple of months away. But I needed gift money, plus the assorted needs of a well-balanced life: beer, gas, CDs, beer, and date money.

I was broke. I'd been fired from my last job after I suffered the tragic loss of my third grandparent in eight weeks.

Now I was on the trail again, filling out apps, pretending to care, shaking hands, and telling lies.

I turned the corner onto Sherman. I knew the town. I knew every business there. One block down Sherman there was a bright yellow light. The bagel place. Why not? Give them a try.

Einstein Bagels. What kind of a genius did you have to be to put cream cheese on a bagel? But the manager there blew me off. And then I was back out on the mean streets.

Papa John's pizza. That's what I wanted. I could drive delivery, make tips, race around town with a little sign on my car, get some mileage money. See inside people's homes. Meet hot, lonely young trophy wives whose creaky old millionaire husbands were off in the city working late.

"It's good to have a rich fantasy life, Christopher," I told myself. "Keeps you from thinking that you're a pizza guy."

Into Papa John's. Out of Papa John's. I was too young. They mostly hired college kids to deliver.

Yeah, that was good thinking, because it's not like college guys are going to be zipping around town faced on frat beer. I'd have said something sarcastic to the manager, but we buy Papa John's at home sometimes, and I didn't want him deciding to blow his nose on my pepperoni.

The hotel? No, those were lifers working there. The bookstores? Geeks, college kids with pierced eyebrows and bad hair. The hot dog place? Not happening. Mickey D's? The brothas worked there.

Fast food was all blacks and Mexicans around here. McDonald's, Burger King, Taco Bell, if you didn't speak Spanish you weren't happening there. Not that it was a huge loss. Not like my secret dream was to stuff burritos at Taco Bell.

I'd come all the way around the block. Back to Church. Looked left. Looked right.

Shoes. I could sell shoes. Me and Al Bundy. That ruined that. I was too young to be Al Bundy.

Okay, think it through. Starbucks? No, David worked at a Starbucks. The Gap? Yeah, right.

Wait. I had walked right by it. The copy place. I could handle that. Make copies. Add toner. Meet hot college girls who wanted me to make copies of their research papers: Why High School Guys Make the Best Lovers.

"Like I said," I told myself, "good to have a rich fantasy life. That way you can avoid realizing that the college kids are pitying you and thinking, 'Oh, man, I better really study or I'll end up like this loser.' "

I went in the door.

"Hi. Can I see the manager?"

"Is something wrong?"

Speaking of losers. He was a little guy. Creepy. His name tag said KEITH. Name tags pretty much never adorn the pockets of society's upper crust.

"No, I was just wondering if you guys were hiring." Yes, it has come to this. I was looking to grab the same job this little twitch held.

Keith shrugged. "You can fill out an app."

He handed me an application. I suppressed the sigh. It was getting late. There had to be something coming on TV.

Just Shoot Me. I was missing David Spade. For this?

I filled out the app. The manager came out after a while, looked me over. Name tag there, too. But his said MR. TRENT. He was not hostile, but not friendly, either.

"Christopher Hitchcock?" he read off the app.

"Yeah. Yes, I mean. That's me."

He was a small guy, too, with a bad comb-over, but he had intense eyes. He stared at me like staring meant something. Like I was supposed to throw up my hands and confess that yes, yes, I intended to steal paper clips.

"What kind of a name is Hitchcock?"

"Uh . . . I don't know."

"Your people. Where are they from?"

I shrugged. "My dad's from Nebraska. My mom's from Naperville."

"Hitchcock. That wasn't changed from anything, was it? Like, you know, Americanized?"

I was about a millimeter away from saying, "Yeah, we changed it from Kwan Lee Ho, can't you tell?" but I didn't. I just said, "No. I don't think so."

He nodded. "You can't be too careful. I mean, this is still America. But it's not all America. You know what I mean."

"Uh-huh."

"Start Saturday, ten in the morning, sharp. I don't tolerate lateness."

"Don't you want to see my references?" I asked this, like an idiot, ignoring the fact that my references were made up.

And then Jalil yelled, "What are you, in a coma? Wake up."

He was a few feet away, trying to grab me and pull me from the tree onto the flat ground. I blinked. I felt blood rush to my cheeks. I was embarrassed and I didn't know why.

He grabbed my arm, I jumped, just as April jumped toward David.

I landed in a heap on top of Jalil.

"Get off me," he said.

I climbed up. Brushed dirt off my knees.

"What were you doing back in the real world? Sleeping over there, too? I'm sitting here going, 'Wake up, wake up' for five minutes. April had to climb around and poke you in the ear."

"I was . . . I was job hunting." I shook off a bad feeling I couldn't quite name. "Sucks."

"Yeah, well, it's no party here," David said. "There are people coming up from behind us. We need to haul."

"What people?" I demanded.

"Who cares what people? You know any people here you want to wait around and say hi to? Come on. Let's move."

It was late afternoon. April and I had wasted the better part of the day sitting cramped and disgruntled, wedged into trees.

The trees had mellowed their "song" throughout the day. Now we barely noticed it. But we kept an ear open because the last time the trees had warned us when some product was about to hit the fan. It made a nature lover of you. If the trees had anything else that worried them, we wanted to hear about it.

"Jalil and I did some reconnaissance, back down the way we came," David announced. "There's some big bunch of people coming from that direction. Maybe a hundred people on some kind of horse-drawn wagons, like. And Hetwan walking with them. That's all we could see."

"That's enough," I agreed. "Let's go be somewhere else."

We set out, trudging along the same path, deeper into Hetwan country. Deeper into the humming trees. David said the guys behind us were moving slowly. No need for us to panic, as long as we kept moving.

The landscape around us changed very little, except that perhaps the trees were taller and the colors and shapes of leaves a little more extreme. As if, out by the borders, this "Lucy in the Sky with Diamonds" forest had wanted to keep it mellow, but now that it was deep within itself it could cut loose.

"You ever go into that copy place?" I asked no one in particular.

"What, Kinko's?" David answered distractedly.

"No, the other one. Not Kinko's. It's not a chain, it's an independent, down by the Chinese place."

"No," David said. "Why?"

"I think I applied for a job there."

"That's good, man," Jalil said. "You're entering the exciting world of high tech. Think they'll let you use the collator?"

"Yeah, it wouldn't compare to your excellent

career of sticking stainless steel skewers up chicken butts at Boston Market," I said.

Jalil laughed. "Hey, they don't let me cook the chickens. I just work the counter and occasionally slice up some birds. You need special training to stick stainless steel skewers up chicken butts."

Everyone laughed. Including me. It was weird talking about the real world as we trudged toward nowhere beneath royal-blue, dagger-shaped leaves that waved atop palm trees.

April started singing. She does this from time to time. The girl is an actress or singer or whatever in the making. Someday when I'm a tired, suit-wearing, stoop-shouldered, briefcase-toting drone climbing down off the METRA to find my nice-but-not-exciting car in the commuter parking lot, April will be Celine Dion.

Which is not a compliment.

"Oh, man, not *Rent,*" I groaned.

April is a drama club person. They're rehearsing *Rent.* Not my personal idea of music. Although if I ever need to drive someone into a terminal depression, I'll buy them the CD.

"It's a great song," April said.

"It's about a crack whore with AIDS. The sun is up, we're not starving or dead. So how about something a little perkier than 'I'm a poor, pitiful crackhead prostitute with AIDS and I'm going to die a miserable death in the gutter but I l-o-o-o-ove you'?"

April flashed me a phony smile. "You have a request? Or do you just want to be unpleasant?"

I thought for a minute. "How about —"

"Not some TV theme song."

"Oh. Okay, do you know any Blink?"

"Christopher, you're an idiot. But I mean that in the nicest possible way. You don't sing punk as you walk along. You need a band. And I'm not talking air guitar."

"Girls don't sing rock anyway," I said, deliberately provoking her. "Girl singers just moan and whine about what jerks men are."

"Strange that would be such a popular theme with women singers," April said dryly. "I mean, how many of them even know you personally?"

Having scored a laugh off me, she said, "Here you go, Christopher. Just for you. But you have to do the rhythmic clapping. . . . 'So no one told you life was gonna be this way.'"

She launched into the theme from *Friends*.

I clapped.

And thus we walked through Ka Anor's forest, carrying a bit of sweet familiarity with us to comfort us amid the weirdness.

Unfortunately, the comforting part ended on the second reprise, when the trees clapped.

No, not their leaves. They just made a clapping sound, at the exact point in the song where they should.

And when April fell suddenly silent, the tune, if not the words, continued.

"The trees are singing the *Friends* song," Jalil said.

"Yeah."

"Imprinting. Like songbirds. Like parrots, maybe."

"That's not too bizarre," I said. "Let's do the *Beverly Hillbillies* next."

The sky was darkening. The sun had set, eliciting a long, long sigh from the trees. And now, in the gathering gloom, as we tried hard not to think about where we were, some alien trees were kind of whispering and shushing about jobs that are a joke and love lives that are DOA.

"Should have let you sing your crackhead song," I muttered. "We could drive Ka Anor back to his own universe."

Now that we were listening, though, we heard other music. Not trees. Instruments. Like flutes a long way off.

And then, closer, laughter.

"Must be those guys we saw behind us," David hissed. "How did they catch up to us?"

"I don't see anything," April said, crouching

instinctively and peering through the widely spaced tree trunks.

"We keep having to detour around the valleys and scoop mountains," Jalil pointed out. "We may not be following a straight line."

"I think they're in that direction," David said, pointing off to what had been our left. "Let's cut away, right angles to their line of march."

"Line of march? Have you been reading Tom Clancy again?"

"Come on, let's go."

David turned and froze. I saw his face and I just knew, absolutely knew that I didn't want to turn around.

I turned around anyway. I was right. I didn't want to see what was behind us.

Four Hetwan stared, silent, their mouth parts working endlessly.

CHAPTER VII

The Hetwan didn't move. But they were armed. I'd never seen them armed before. These were carrying what looked like short spears, broad at the base, swooping to a needlelike point. The weapons were maybe two feet long, brown and translucent, like they were made out of the same plastic they use to make guitar picks.

David drew his sword from its scabbard. Jalil unclasped the Swiss Army knife with the tiny but inhumanly sharp Coo-Hatch blade. April tightened her grip on the backpack that held a bottle of Advil, a CD player, and about two big handfuls of diamonds.

Me, I just stared. Stared and wished, not for the first time, that I had a machine gun, if not a tank.

"Come with us, trespassers," one of the Hetwan said in a whispery voice.

"We didn't mean to trespass," David said reasonably. "Show us the way out of your lands and we'll go immediately."

"Come with us," the Hetwan said.

"No."

The Hetwan stared, and for this fragile moment, I had hope. Maybe they'd just let us go.

Then they took their two-foot daggers or spears or whatever they were and inserted the thicker end into their fringed, creepy mouths.

The three grasping mouth parts locked on with audible snaps that sounded uncomfortably like gun hammers being cocked.

David raised the sword, point toward the Hetwan: a warning, a threat.

"This doesn't have to get ugly," David said.

One of the Hetwan spit. It came out through the end of the mouth-spear. A spitwad. A fast spitwad.

The spit landed on the ground, just between David's feet. Perfectly between David's feet.

The ground, the dirt itself, began to burn.

David jumped back. Raised his sword high, ready to attack.

A second Hetwan spit. The loogie caught the

blade of the sword, about midpoint between hilt and point.

A one-inch semicircle burned. Steel itself, burning. And then the flame died and a neat notch had been cut into the blade.

The Hetwan had just burned dirt and steel. I had a pretty clear idea what that same venom would do to my face.

"I have an idea: Let's go with the Hetwan. Since they asked so nicely and all."

David hesitated. I could see the wheels turning in his head. He knew we were beat. He just thought maybe we should take a bit more punishment before we gave in. You know, for the sake of honor.

I was mad at David. I don't know why, exactly. And I was scared. But I was less scared of surrendering than I was of feeling my nose melting and burning.

"Hey, I surrender," I told the Hetwan. I raised my shaky hands nice and high, palms out to show I was unarmed.

My action pretty much forced David's hand. He lowered his sword and slammed it back in its sheath.

One of the Hetwan unscrewed his portable venom SuperSoaker and said, "You will follow us."

Just that. Not, "Give us the sword and the knife." They were leaving us armed. Big mistake. Unless it wasn't and they just weren't very worried about us.

Two of the Hetwan moved around behind us, glidey-sliding on their sticky pads. Two led the way.

Then salvation came as quickly as despair. The trees set up their eerie keening again.

"Wood chippers," Jalil said.

"Same song," April agreed. "I think they're coming this way."

David spoke in a low monotone, trying not to convey emotion, as if the Hetwan all spoke French and all we had to do to fool them was not get emotional. "When they appear, soon as they come in sight, everyone run as far as you can, then drop. Soon as they're past, up and run."

"The Hetwan look too calm," Jalil pointed out.

He was right. This was their country. They must know what the howling trees were about.

Sure enough, just as the trees reached hysterical pitch, the three still-armed Hetwan unscrewed their SuperSoakers and let out a howl like nothing I'd ever heard before.

It started high, so high that dogs all the way back in the real world were probably yapping in response. But the sound dropped swiftly down, lower, lower, till they reached a pleasant Sheryl Crow, at which point they started what could only be a song.

There were no words, at least none that I understood. Maybe they were speaking some foreign language. (Like English was their native tongue.) Anyway, it seemed like a song, and a kind of pretty one, too, although the notes all sounded a little off.

The nearest trees stopped their own mad howling. And the sound of the wood chippers seemed to swerve away.

I was amazed and depressed by all this. April seemed entranced. Jalil was shaking his head, annoyed that once again Everworld refused to behave in any way sanctioned by his physics textbook.

Fortunately David remained David, bless his crazy little heart.

I heard the sound of drawn steel. A whoosh of air as the blade came down fast, not six inches from my face, swept into a horizontal slash, and passed neatly through the scrawny necks of the two Ally McBugs behind us.

The two front Hetwan jerked around and scrambled for their face needles. David caught one with an upswing that opened the bug up from where his unit would be, if he had a unit, to his shoulder. Green and gray and purple insides spilled out onto the ground.

The last Hetwan just stood there. He knew he didn't have time to load up his weapon and fire. He just stood there. Stared at us with his huge fly eyes, mouth parts still working.

He knew he was toast. He knew he was the cockroach in the Raid commercial. But David hesitated.

"Do you surrender?" David demanded, pointing the sword right at the Hetwan's mouth.

"I serve Ka Anor. My death is irrelevant," the creature said calmly.

"Yeah?" David asked. Then he lunged, buried half the sword in the Hetwan's chest, yanked it back out, and watched the bug drop.

It was cold. It was necessary.

David's face was a clouded mirror of my own horror. They were aliens, they were just bugs, but they had been alive, and now they weren't.

"Oh, God," April moaned softly. She covered her mouth and stepped back. Her heel hit one of the Hetwan heads and sent it rolling sluggishly. The mouthparts were still moving slowly, slower, slower.

David wiped his blade on grass. It looked like a

calm, deliberate thing to do. It wasn't. He wiped too long. He wanted it off. He didn't want to be reminded of it later.

He had the creeps, no question. But there were other levels to David. What he'd just done made him sick. It also gave him a rush.

Jalil finally got him, shook his shoulder, snapped him out of his trance. David sheathed the sword. The notch was gone. The sword had healed itself.

We started moving again, this time through almost pitch-dark. Night had fallen on Hetwan country. The trees were no longer singing, and neither were we.

No moon. No stars. At least not that we could see. Was that because the Hetwan didn't have a moon in their little patch of Everworld? Or was it just cloudy?

The result was the same: darkness like black velvet wrapped around your head.

Nothing makes you feel more helpless than not being able to see. You stand there, muscles tensed, back and neck tingling as you wait for something you're never even going to see to chop you, hit you, rip you.

The sound of your own breathing becomes the most compelling thing around. Breathe in, breathe out. You can hear the fear in your own breathing. Then you notice your heart. And you notice the watery ache of muscles that have been tensed and ready for too long. And breathe. And breathe in the night air.

We stumbled around, unable to make out anything but dim outlines. At any moment we could all four walk off into one of the ice-cream-scoop holes. Or lose contact with one another. Or wander into whatever other nocturnal nastiness Hetwan country might hold.

Too easy to imagine that those big Hetwan bug eyes could see through the dark like a Delta team with night-vision goggles on. Too easy to imagine that the four of us were luminescent targets as brightly lit up as Tom Hanks arriving for Oscar night.

Then we saw light. It flickered, golden, through the trees. Torches, maybe. The light was reflected in mirrored leaves, turned into a thousand distant fireflies.

"We can move closer to the light, figure out which way it's moving, get behind it, and follow them," Jalil suggested. "That way we'll know a safe path."

"Or we could just crash right here and sleep," April said.

"That sounds good to me," I said. Curl up in the blind-man darkness and run away to the real world till the sun came up in Hetwan country. Best of a lousy situation. I searched for

David in the utter gloom. "How about you, general?"

"We're not going anywhere special, so I guess there's no hurry," David said.

Maybe I'd misjudged him. Maybe he felt worse about the Great Hetwan Massacre than I thought. Or maybe he just figured that was the way he had to play it.

I didn't want David to be doubting his instincts. I wanted him all razor edged and hyper if I was going to sleep.

"Sleep," I announced. "By a vote of three to one. Jalil is in the minority. Better call up Jesse Jackson and Reverend Al and have a demonstration. White folks imposing sleep on a brotha."

It was a joke. Obviously.

Jalil didn't seem to think so. "Hey, Christopher, maybe it's crosses they're burning over there. Trot on over, see if they have a spare sheet for you."

"Excuse me for thinking you had a sense of humor, Jalil."

David snapped, "Damn it, Christopher, can you just cut out that crap? I mean, what are you, just stupid? You're here in the deep weeds with a black man and a Jew, and you're a racist, an anti-Semite? How smart is that?"

That made me mad. I had been joking. I'd been kidding. Now David was siding with Jalil, who was just mad because his brilliant plan had been voted down. And now, suddenly, because of some joke I was in the KKK?

"Screw both of you," I muttered. "Excuse me, all three of you, because don't forget, I'm a sexist, too."

I settled down on the ground and grabbed one of the tattered food bags we'd been carrying. I stuffed a small loaf of bread in my mouth and tried not to think about how thirsty I was because Jalil was carrying the water bottle and I sure as hell wasn't going to ask him for it.

Then I started thinking how cold my back would be once I laid down in the dirt. And then I tried not to think about what kinds of insects there might be, or predators, or snakes.

I was just mad now. Scared and mad. And tired and frustrated. And thirsty, which just added torture to everything else.

"The three of you don't have one sense of humor between you," I said bitterly. "Give me the water."

I heard Jalil moving. Looking for me, to hand me the water. His foot found my hand, crushed the clenched fingers.

"Hey!"

"What?"

"What do you mean, 'what'? You stepped on my hand."

"I didn't see it."

Then I did something dumb. I shoved at the place where I thought his leg was. I hit his knee with the palm of my squashed hand. It had to hurt me worse than it did him, but he was on me before I knew what was what.

I started rabbit-punching, blind. He was doing the same. I think I was hitting his side, I felt ribs against my knuckles. He was hitting my stomach, but he didn't have much leverage.

"Get off me!" I yelled.

We were both grunting and punching and grappling and now there was a new set of hands yanking on me, fumbling, pulling on me, finding my neck and hauling back.

I gasped, choked, eyes filled with tears, blood pounding in my ears and face. Then Jalil hit me in the cheek and stars exploded in the darkness.

I heard David yell, "Jalil, stop it. I have him, stop it."

I was loose, rolling free. Dazed.

"I'll kill you!" I yelled, voice rasped rough.

"Nobody move," David hissed. I heard the sound of his sword coming out of its sheath. "Both of you: Stop right where you are."

"He broke my cheek, ——"

"They're going to hear us. You're going to get us all killed."

"Too late," April said.

My heart sank. I had the sudden, utter clarity of knowing that I'd done something deeply stupid. Although in my mind it was still Jalil's fault.

I looked around, and now there was light. Not much, and at first I wondered if it was just the 'stars 'n' Tweety Birds' cartoon effect from getting hit with a solid right.

But no, this was no illusion. It was an angel, or as close as I hope to see in this life.

My first thought, my first flash was that it was a beautiful woman. And despite having a rapidly swelling face, and despite being scared peeless, and despite being enraged at Jalil and David and April, too, though she hadn't exactly done or said anything, I was excited. Attracted.

The angel was beautiful, with a face dominated by immense, lustrous green eyes and framed by golden ringlets, and with a bow mouth and full lips and brilliant white teeth.

And only then, only after I had felt that first rush of improbable carnal lust, did it occur to me that this angel was a man.

"Good evening," he said in a voice that made April's best singing voice sound like the Budweiser frogs. "I am called Ganymede. I have been sent to invite you to join our revels."

IX

The four of us just stared.

He was tall, but not Loki tall. Not intimidating in the least. He was very near to being naked. His only clothing was a white loincloth kind of thing that looked as though it might slip off his narrow hips at any moment.

You could see every muscle beneath his lustrous skin, but he was not muscular, not muscle-bound, not some steroid case. He was thin but not emaciated.

When he moved, you felt his restrained power. He looked as if he could walk through a brick wall. And he looked like he'd step aside to avoid squashing a bug.

I shot a sidelong glance at David. He was staring, mouth open, his brows drawn close in an expression of anxiety. It made him look remarkably stupid. Jalil kept swallowing nervously.

April gaped at Ganymede with frank, open admiration and blatant hunger. It was pathetic. She was drooling.

David said, "Yes, sir, but aren't there, um, you know, Hetwan over there?"

"There are," Ganymede said. His eyes dropped in regret. "Indeed, they purposed to do you some harm, I believe, but Dionysus has prevailed upon them to allow you to join our happy band."

"So . . ." Jalil began, faded out, and restarted. "So, you're saying the Hetwan will kill us unless we agree to come over voluntarily to the, you know, to your party."

Ganymede stepped close. He laid his hand on Jalil's arm. "Put such gloomy thoughts aside. There is food. There is wine. There is love. Come, and let us all eat and drink and be merry."

"'For tomorrow we shall die,'" April said, finishing the famous quote.

Ganymede seemed surprised. "Yes. As you say, we must eat, drink, and be merry, for tomorrow we shall die."

"You can quote me on that," April said dryly.

"What do we do?" I asked.

"Look behind you," Jalil said.

I did. Ganymede gave off a faint light, a glow-in-the-dark thing that only barely illuminated the Hetwan who had moved in behind us. How many Hetwan, I didn't know, couldn't see. But enough. Did they know we'd killed four of their homies? They must.

"All right, then," I said. "Let's party."

The bright-lit procession was farther than it seemed once you accounted for a detour around one of the ice-cream-sundae mountains and an even more nerve-racking trip skirting the edge of a valley.

We followed Ganymede. The Hetwan moved silently behind us. I still wanted to call a time-out to return Jalil's punch. I was still pissed at him. I mean, I tried to get along with Jalil, but any little joke and I was the bad guy all of a sudden.

But I was distracted from all that by the fact that my field of vision was filled with Ganymede.

"So, you're a god, right?" I asked him as I tried not to look at his smooth, muscular back and barely clothed, cheeks-on-display butt.

"I am cupbearer to the gods of Olympus," he said. "I am immortal, but only by the charity of great Zeus. I was born a mortal man."

"You got promoted? I didn't know you could do that."

"I was a young man of Troy. I was playing in the fields with my friends when Zeus looked down and saw me. In his eyes I was beautiful. So he changed himself into a great eagle and flew down from Olympus to become my lover."

That brought about thirty seconds of dense silence.

"Zeus is gay?" I asked.

April shushed me.

I said, "April, don't start in with me, okay? Someone had to ask."

"Zeus is a god," Ganymede said. "The greatest of the gods, lord of Olympus."

"He's, like, married to Hera, though," Jalil said.

"Zeus has had several wives and many, many consorts."

"And he has a bunch of children," Jalil pointed out. "Hercules is his son, isn't he?"

"Great Zeus has many children," Ganymede confirmed. And now he sounded a little peeved. "Zeus is father to Athena, Ares, Hephaistos, the Graces, Hermes, Apollo, the Muses, Artemis, and yes, Heracles. But you would think Heracles was his only child. Every time I speak with mortals it's much the same: 'Do you know Heracles? What's he like? Is he really that strong?' No one ever asks about Apollo. But he . . . Now, he is a god."

I dropped back a couple of steps, hopefully out of Ganymede's hearing. Back to walk beside David. David and I didn't always get along, but being close to David didn't bother me. Being close to Ganymede did. Not that I'm one of those guys who hates gays. I mean, to each his own, right? Just not around me. That's all I'm saying.

Still, despite being pretty open-minded, Ganymede made me jumpy. For one thing, in the normal world I was maybe, I don't know, maybe like a nine or at least an eight on the scale of guy looks. But compared to Ganymede I was Fat Bastard, Homer Simpson, and Ed Asner all rolled into one.

"Okay, this is weird," I whispered to David. "We're getting mythology lessons from an immortal pretty boy."

"Uh-huh," David said. He seemed distracted. He was, in fact, following Ganymede closely with his eyes.

"Hey, you don't want to make Senna jealous," I said.

David flared and grabbed a handful of my shirt. "What are you talking about?"

I shoved his hand away. "Take it easy. You were checking him out, dude."

"Screw you, Christopher. I am not gay."

"Yeah? I'm not, either. Not even slightly."

"You sure?" he hissed. "You were moving up close to him. Maybe that's why Senna dumped you, man."

"What are you trying to say?"

"What are you trying to say?" he echoed.

I took a deep breath. Okay, this was getting too intense. This was so not the time.

David said, "I was not checking him out, jerk-wad."

"Me neither," I said.

We fell silent. An uneasy peace. We walked along and tried not to look at the only source of light in a million miles of darkness.

"You know . . ."

"What?" David snapped, on guard instantly.

"Nothing. Nothing. I'm just thinking Hera must not be much to look at if Zeus is going after a guy. I mean, what's that about? Zeus, man, he must have all the babes he can handle. So what's this about?"

"You know what, let's just drop it, all right?" David said. "We have important things to focus on: the Hetwan. And whatever is going on up ahead there. You think just because this guy is swish and sounds nice and looks, you know, you think that means he's not a possible enemy?"

"Look at Jalil, man. He's hanging on every word. You think Jalil . . . ? He's definitely checking him out."

"I hate this place," David muttered.

"So what's the plan, general?"

"I don't know. Shut up, I'll figure something out when we get up there."

April dropped back to join us.

"That is the best-looking male creature I have ever seen," she said in a whisper.

"You think so?" I said nonchalantly.

"You didn't notice. Uh-huh," she said skeptically.

"He's a guy," David said, as though that would make everything perfectly clear and beyond question.

"A guy? A guy? He's like, he's like, like what Michelangelo had in mind when he tried to paint or sculpt perfect male beauty. He's the ideal every woman has buried deep in her subconscious, the guy she knows, no matter what, no matter who she is, no matter anything, married, boyfriend, wouldn't matter, she'd say yes. Look at him, he's perfect."

"Yeah. Too bad he's gay, huh?" I said.

April sighed. "Hey, Christopher, now you have it all, the Bigot's Big Four: blacks, Jews, women, and gays."

"Not the same," David muttered inaudibly, almost coming to my defense.

"Uh-huh. You guys are so obsessed with acting tough and being all macho and all that caveman stuff you can't even let yourselves appreciate pure beauty when you see it. You have to turn it into a sexual thing, a challenge to your manhood. What's the problem, feeling like you may want to . . . cross over?" She laughed her mocking laugh and in the darkness I flushed.

"Uh-huh, but it's not a sexual thing for you, right, April? Talking about how you'd say yes, and all?"

"Well, I was joking. I don't believe in premarital sex."

"You're kidding."

"No, I'm not kidding, Christopher. Sorry to complicate your little fantasies, sweetheart, but I believe in sex within marriage." She took a deep breath and blew it out slowly. "I'm just saying, when I see that particular, immortal, glow-in-the-dark butt I think I'm ready for marriage. Look at those cheeks."

"No," David grated.

"What cheeks?" I said.

"Ah," April said, all mock-wise. "I see the problem."

"There's no damned problem," David snapped.

April laughed, which made me really mad. And I'd have told her so, but we had at last arrived at the party.

CHAPTER X

A close-up look at the procession wiped unnerving images of Ganymede from my mind. Mostly.

The procession comprised about two hundred people. And I use the term *people* very loosely. There were satyrs, there were nymphs, there were fairies and, yes, there were mortals.

Most of these folks were arrayed on a series of huge wagons. Trailers or platforms on wheels, each drawn by a dozen or more magnificent horses. Some of the platforms were no bigger than a boxing ring. Others were as wide and as long as the average suburban house lot.

The platforms — there were six in all — were piled with silk pillows on which lolled dark blue and light green and pale yellow nymphs, hairy, goat-legged satyrs, and a lot of guys, who covered the range from *GQ* smooth and sophisticated to World Wrestling Federation beefy and loud.

And there were women. It was as if someone had invited the Hawaiian Tropic girls, the Victoria's Secret models, and the last five casts of *Baywatch* to the annual Convention of Impossibly Hot Women.

There was food. Overflowing baskets of ripe fruit, dripping honey, silver platters loaded with steaming-hot roasts, skewers dripping beef fat, chicken legs, turkey legs, and legs off something that looked like it could probably eat turkeys for a snack.

Plus, there was wine. Red wine, white wine, pink wine. Wine in big vats, wine in wineskins, wine in buckets, wine in goblets, wine spilling down chins and staining what few clothing items were in evidence.

Every fairy, every nymph, every satyr, every guy, every babe was drunk. Screaming, giggling, babbling, roaring, yahooing, stumbling, slipping, falling-off-the-slow-moving-platforms drunk.

Some were dancing in a sort of manic way, dancing to music that may have been bad music or may have just been badly played, but either way was definitely not anything a sober person would appreciate.

And in the midst of the largest platform lolled

a god. He was an older guy. His head was partly bald, and the hair around the sides was white. He had the red, pitted, Rudolph nose of a confirmed alcoholic, bleary, unfocused eyes, and a smile that reminded me of Alfred E. Neuman.

"Dionysus," Ganymede said.

"God of great parties?" I suggested.

"God of all altered states of mind," Ganymede said fondly. "But most officially, god of wine."

I had met some gods in Everworld. Loki, Huitzilopoctli, and Hel. I had formed a negative impression, based on the fact that each of these gods had been interested in killing me.

One look at Dionysus and I knew he was different. Dionysus was a cool god. As cool as an old guy can be, anyway.

A woman screamed. You know, one of those "I am so drunk" screams. And then she lurched, blew chunks off the back rail of Dionysus's platform, and toppled off the side.

I flinched at the sound of flesh and bone hitting dirt. But moments later she was hefted up by three straining Hetwan and replaced on the platform, where she revived and rejoined the party.

The Hetwan were very helpful that way. They trailed along on all sides of each platform. I saw a sort of flying wedge of them chopping down trees that blocked the way.

There was no question that despite the wild parties, the silent Hetwan were in charge. And if I'd had any doubts about that, the chain fastened loosely around Dionysus's throat would have made it all clear.

"They're taking him to Ka Anor," I said.

Ganymede looked down at me, and there were tears in his hypnotic eyes. "Yes. We go to Ka Anor. Dionysus and I. We go to learn of the great mystery which once, long ago, as a mortal, I understood. But that I have long put aside from my thoughts."

"What mystery?"

"The mystery of death," he said. Then he smiled. "So eat, drink, be merry. For tomorrow, when we reach the city of Ka Anor, we shall all surely die."

The Hetwan made us get up on Dionysus's platform. A couple of the bugs lifted me under the arms. It gave me the screaming heebie-jeebies. Didn't these guys know we'd smoked four of their boys? Didn't they care?

But, getting past the way-too-numerous Hetwan, I've definitely been worse places than this rolling party. A nymph the color of deep water handed me a gold goblet filled with red wine. I took a long swig. Why not? I didn't exactly like our chances. The Hetwan had a god and an immortal under control, so I figured we weren't going to be busting out. So why not drink?

Come to think of it, why not do any number of things, all of which were more fun than fighting the Hetwan? An hour with a matched pair of nymphs would clear my mind of Ganymede.

With a scream, a blond in a wonderfully loose toga landed against me, knocked me back onto a cloud of pillows, and kissed me on the lips.

"Get off him," David snapped. He reached down, grabbed the girl by the arm, and yanked her off me.

"What is your problem?!" I yelled.

"We're on our way to Ka Anor, you really think you need to be getting drunk and laid?"

I nodded. "Actually, that's exactly what I think I need to be doing."

A satyr lurched up behind April, reached around, and grabbed two handfuls.

"Hey!" She swung an elbow straight back over her shoulder and nailed his goateed head with an Oscar De La Hoya.

The satyr shook his head, stunned, then evidently forgot who he was chasing and went off after the bleached blond.

David grabbed Jalil and pulled him close, forming the four of us into a little huddle of hopeless buzz-killers.

"You know, you're a real puritan, David. Don't drink, don't screw around. You and April. How did I ever get hooked up with you people? Not to mention Jalil, the only black man in history who can't party."

David dropped down beside me, kneeling on only one knee because the sword got in the way. He grabbed my collar. Big mistake. I slapped his hand away. He let it go, but he didn't back off.

"You listen up, Christopher. Everyone is tired of your crap, okay? Sick of it. Sick of the black this, and the Jew that, and mostly sick of you dragging along like this is all someone else's problem, not yours. Lose the attitude."

"I think you mean 'lose the attitude, *mister.*' I mean, that's how my dad always says it. And you know, I think of you as my daddy away from home, David."

He glared at me. There was a muscle twitching in his cheek. He looked like that guy on *The Practice,* all dark and intense and unshaven.

"We're a team, like it or not, Christopher. It's us against them. We don't have time for us against us."

"David, does it ever occur to you how full of it you actually are? There's no 'us.' We're not the Dallas Cowboys, David, we're not even the Cubbies. We're an accident. You and I aren't friends, you and Jalil aren't friends, and as for April, all I want to do with her is get busy. That's me."

I grabbed a passing glass of wine. Not hard to

do since wine was constantly passing. But this glass came from the hand of the cupbearer himself. Ganymede looked down, his green eyes so serious. I took the glass, looked away, and then he was gone.

"You're a pathetic excuse for a man," David sneered.

"David, if Senna were here you'd be her sock puppet. Don't lecture me. You're all tough and bad and Clint Eastwood when she's not around, but when she is you're just her tool."

That got him, I was pleased to see. He blinked several times. I took a deep drink.

Jalil and April now knelt down, too, and we formed a little kneeling conspiracy corner, surrounded by the party Caligula only wished he could throw.

"The question is, how do we get out of here?" Jalil said. "It has to be better to take our chances here than it is to wait till we're in Ka Anor's palace, or whatever he has."

"Dude, we're in the middle of an alien forest, at night, surrounded by aliens." I laughed and drained the cup. Awfully good wine, it was. Awfully good. It sent a pleasurable buzz all through my teeny-tiny capillaries.

Weird, actually. It wasn't that much wine. But

it was hitting me pretty fast. I felt like I'd killed a six-pack.

I looked past the ever-so-serious faces of my fellow "team members" at the wild, self-contained little world around me.

It was a metaphor, that's what it was. Or was it an analogy? Mmm. I didn't know. Anyway, it was me, in the light, but all surrounded by darkness and danger. Wine and sex and music and laughter and death coming up in the future and maybe even sooner if I pissed off the Hetwan enough.

It was like life, man. Party today. Party and don't think about the Ka Anor thing. You know, whatever the Ka Anor thing would be in, like, in . . .

Point is, party, man. That was the point.

April was saying something to me. Good-looking girl, April. Wouldn't mind, but hey, if she was gonna be all, you know . . . Then forget it, right?

Plenty of fish in the sea. Who said that? Someone. Babes all around me. Wine. More wine, that's what I needed. David's face kind of wiggly now. Kind of all serious, but kind of drifting, too. And Jalil was . . .

Then he was gone. All three of them were gone. Stomped off. The party had surged, crashed around us like hurricane surf. Where were they? Gone, man. Thought we were a team and all.

Someone touching me. Nice. Kissing. Mmm-hmmm. The vino, gulp, gulp, gulp.

Man, way too drunk. I was drunk enough to . . . Try to stand, Christopher, that's how you can tell if you're too . . .

Yep, you're drunk.

But now I couldn't see the women anymore. I mean, I could see them, but they were like, I don't know. Saw through them. Shapes. Movement. But they were kind of dim, and all I really saw was the old man, the old god. Dionysus laughing.

He was shining right through all the others. Big old bald head thrown back, mouth wide, haw, haw, haw, haw. But I could look straight through women and men and satyrs and nymphs, and oh, God, oh God, they were all fake.

Nothing was real but the laughing god guzzling the wine and leering around at his own fantasy.

No, he wasn't the only real thing. Ganymede was there, too, if I turned around to look.

My friends. The other members of Your Dallas Cowboys, starting lineup. David. April. Jalil. They were there, jostling the illusions. One of them, one of the wraith women, one of those luscious ghosts was kissing Jalil, weakening his resolve, I could see it. An illusion had an unreal tongue so far down Jalil's throat she'd be licking his liver soon.

The laughter echoed dimly, like I was hearing it from the wrong end of a long hallway. The music was a faint wail. Even the wine, which had been everywhere, rich and red, the color of blood, now was revealed as pale and watery.

All but the brilliant glass in my hand. The glass that had been given to me by Ganymede himself.

But more and more I saw Dionysus. And he saw me. He looked right at me. Right through the party. A stare that cut through all the bull, a stare, weird, man, weird, a stare that looked past his own bleary eyes, ignored his own red, happy face, a stare that was from somewhere else, like there was a whole different god using Dionysus as a mask.

The wine. My wine. From the hand of Ganymede.

Silence. No sound now, not the wind in the trees, not the creak of the platform, not the glidey-slidey steps of the very real Hetwan, not the snuffling of the horses, not the giddy, hysterical, forced mirth of the party.

Only one sound. The clank of chain links. The clank of the chain that held Dionysus bound like a dog.

And then, Dionysus spoke, and his mouth didn't move, and I heard the words in my blood, in my heart, in my muscles and bones.

"Save me," Dionysus said. "Save me, mortal, and I will make you a god."

Chapter XII

Then a woosh of noise, like I'd stepped out of a soundproof room into the midst of Puffy's Millennium Party. The music, the girls, the guys, the aliens, the freaks, all real again, real flesh and real loud and overwhelming.

I stood up. My head was perfectly clear. I saw Dionysus, giggling at the antics of a nymph, a satyr, and what looked a lot like a bathtub full of wine.

I saw David fending off some Miss October wanna-be. I saw Jalil not quite fending off another. I saw April chatting with Ganymede and doing the look-away checkout, as bad as any guy. Every time the young god's eyes left April's, hers were doing a quick scan. She'd do this little shudder, this little, "he's so fine" shiver.

"Okay, be cool," I told myself. "Can't let the Hetwan know. Act cool. Act casual."

I grabbed the arm of a staggeringly faced nymph who bore a resemblance to the young Winona Ryder and, carrying her along with me as cover, I made my way through the mayhem. I dropped her off when I reached David.

I took David's arm. Squeezed his bicep, stuck a big dumb grin on my face, and said, "It's all bull, man."

"Go have another drink," he said and dismissed me.

"Listen to me. Don't look like you're listening to me, but listen to me anyway." I guess my tone of voice made an impression.

"What is it?"

"This is all fake: the babes, the freaks, the wine, the whole thing. The platform is real, the horses are real, we're real, Ganymede and Dionysus are real. And unfortunately the Hetwan are real. But the rest of this is just Dionysus's little fun house."

"How drunk are you?"

"Stone-cold sober, and it's a pity. But I was drunk. Ganymede slipped me something. I heard Dionysus talk to me."

"Man, you are drunk. Wasting my time."

"David, listen to me, listen to me or I swear I will have to personally kill you, you arrogant, pompous little self-appointed Napoleon. Do I sound drunk? Am I slurring my words?"

He narrowed his eyes. "No."

"He wants us to save him."

"Yeah? Well, I want him to save us."

"The Hetwan think all this is real. They have him chained down somehow, who knows, some magic chain or whatever. But anyway, he's got them believing this party is real."

I had reached David. I saw the wheels begin to turn in his fevered brain. He was calculating. Good. That was a start.

"Get to Dionysus," David said. "Get close. See what he can tell you. I'll talk to April and Jalil." Then, petulant, "I don't know what Dionysus thinks we can do."

I party-surfed toward Dionysus. Not easy. If there was ever a party I wanted to dive into, this was it. If you added up the sum total of every wild Hollywood party going back to the days of silent films, all the way to the present day, subtracted all the boring stuff, distilled what was left over into pure essence of debauched good times, you still wouldn't beat this party.

Dionysus knew how to party. Even if it was all in his own head. I mean, you think about it, is it really so wrong to drink imaginary wine and play toga tag with imaginary nymphs?

It didn't matter, I guess. Dionysus wanted out, and we wanted out, and that's what mattered.

Besides, I reassured myself, *if we bust him out, he can still use his powers to create a party.*

So I stiff-armed a pair of Britneys and a Moesha or two and I pushed away yet another glass of vino, and I haw-hawed and giggled and grinned my happy-go-lucky way over to Dionysus. I staggered, stumbled, and landed in the corrupt old fart's lap. I lolled back and gazed up, laughing into his laugh, and whispered, "So, how do we get out of here? Can't you just give the Hetwan a shot of god power?"

He made a show of laughing and kept his big, thick-featured face nice and rosy red. As though he were talking to a passing guy, he said, "My powers are only the powers of wine and women and song. I create the joy and abandon of drunken revel."

"Do the Hetwan drink?"

"No, they do not, the barbarians. However . . ."

"They like the ladies?"

He grinned and burst out laughing, keeping up the show for any observant Hetwan. "These are all male Hetwan, priests of a sort. Servants of Ka Anor. Absolutely loyal. Incorruptible. And yet, they have the universal hunger."

"For what, pizza?" He didn't get it.

"Ganymede!" he bellowed. "My cup runs dry!"

Ganymede headed our way, leaving April to follow him with her eyes and shake her head regretfully. I spotted David moving in on her, talking to her in an intense way. The boy could single-handedly kill the cumulative buzz of the entire population of Jamaica on a Saturday night.

"Let me refill your glass, great Dionysus," Ganymede said, and sure enough, he began pouring.

"Tell this mortal about the Hetwan. What you saw."

Ganymede nodded very slightly. "I was captured before Dionysus. Six days ago, at the farthest frontier of Hetwan country. It was on the second day of my captivity that I witnessed the Hetwan engage in unusual acts."

I bit my tongue to keep from making a joke about unusual acts as they might relate to Ganymede.

"Hetwan females appeared. I say females, but I do not know if that's what they were. I can only say that following their appearance the Hetwan gave birth. And that during the appearance of these . . . these females, the Hetwan were like wild beasts."

I thought that over. So, the Hetwan were horn dogs. Hard to imagine what would qualify as hot-looking by Hetwan standards, but I try to keep an open mind about that kind of stuff.

Dionysus waved Ganymede away. I sat up. The old god looked me straight in the eye. "I can make the Hetwan believe they are being visited by their females. Ganymede says they are as frenzied as a pack of satyrs chasing Aphrodite's handmaidens. While the barbarians are distracted, you must free me from this chain and effect our escape."

I just stared at him. "Kind of a skimpy plan, isn't it?"

"I can give you immortality," he said. "You will live forever, like Ganymede."

"Can you give me his body? Because if I had his body I'd want to live forever. There isn't a mortal woman alive who'd —"

"Isn't immortality enough?"

"What about my friends?"

"Gods, all gods. Minor, of course. It is simply a matter of telling Zeus what you have done to save his favorite."

"Ganymede?"

"Me!" Dionysus cried. "Everyone knows how close Zeus and I are." He held up two fingers and tried to twine them together. He was too drunk to pull it off. He set down his cup and laboriously twisted his pudgy fingers together. "We're like this, Zeus and I."

"Yeah? I heard it was Ganymede and Zeus who were like that. Look, don't you two have any superpowers? I mean, getting past your ability to make parties appear out of thin air? Can't you do the thunderbolt thing?"

"No, that's Zeus."

"Great. So you're deadweight."

Ganymede leaned closer. "We can show you the way to safety. We can take you to Olympus."

At this point David sidled up. He was trying to seem like a happy, drunken party boy and it was pitiful to see. Like watching your parents try to "get down and boogie."

"You know, David, it works better if you pull the stick out of your butt first," I offered helpfully. "Dionysus here says he can make us immortal, plus lead us out of Hetwan country. But we have to save him and Ganymede, and we have to do it without much help from them, aside from a distraction involving unusual acts."

David shot a look at Ganymede.

"No. Hetwan sex," I clarified.

"Which is what?"

I shrugged.

Dionysus let his hand drop to the chain fastened around his throat. "This would have to be cut."

"May as well die trying to get free as go to our deaths with all this," David said, waving a hand to encompass the party.

I looked around at the barrels and buckets of booze and the large numbers of fantastically pretty and exceedingly available women. "Yeah, David. Better to die."

I swear he did not realize I was being sarcastic.

It took another twenty minutes to get all the planning done. It's amazing how much effort can go into plotting your own painful death.

The Hetwan showed no sign of being onto us. Hardly surprising, they weren't really all that familiar with humans.

Jalil maneuvered close to Dionysus. Jalil had Excalibur, his teeny-tiny pocketknife with the Coo-Hatch steel blade that'll cut anything. Even, we hoped, the chain that bound Dionysus.

April was at the front of the wagon with Ganymede. They were going to grab the horses.

David? Well, David was midway between Dionysus and the front of the wagon, ready to do sword tricks on any Hetwan who interfered.

My job was to help drag Dionysus to the

horses. The theory being that I had the most experience with drunks.

David gave me the "ready" nod. I looked at Jalil. He looked sick. Which was reassuring, cause I felt sick.

"Okay, do it," I said to Dionysus.

"One more glass?"

"Do it!" Jalil snapped.

Suddenly, from out of the trees came a rush of wings. The light of the party, Dionysus's own magical light, illuminated a nightmare.

They were bags of organs. That's what they looked like, like translucent bags of organs and blood and guts. Like white balloons filled with the parts of the cow that only French people eat. Fat sausages stuffed with gore.

They were each perhaps two feet across, with amazingly long, dragonfly wings. Sacks of guts with gossamer wings.

They had Hetwan eyes and Hetwan wings, but aside from that I'd never have guessed they were Hetwan. I'd never have guessed they were anything that could exist outside the computers of Industrial Light and Magic.

Forty or fifty of them came swooping toward us, out of the treetops.

I reminded myself: They're not real. They're no

more real than any of the illusions Dionysus had created.

But, man, the Hetwan bought it. They rushed, tripped over one another, leaped up to snatch at passing, swooping females. Their little mouth parts were going hyper.

Jalil sliced. The Coo-Hatch steel cut the chain as if it were made of braided string cheese.

Dionysus started to get up. I had the impression the guy had not stood erect for weeks. I rushed to grab an arm.

The Hetwan began yowling, a hideous, hungry screech, leaping and grabbing at the still-unreached females who were coming back over for a victory roll.

Dionysus straightened his toga and tried to waddle toward the front of the wagon. The partyers magically made way for us, but still it was slow going. Dionysus was about John-Goodman size and about Robert-Downey-Jr.-level stoned. He was weaving back and forth like a toddler taking his first steps.

Jalil and I each had an arm. But we were straining. I was losing my affection for the Partyer-in-Chief.

Then I stopped cold. A couple of the Hetwan had snagged a female. They were ripping her apart with their mouth parts. Ripping open the bag of guts while the female's wings spasmed.

I moaned. Dionysus cast a weary glance at the scene. "Barbarians. No appreciation of the true joys of revelry."

I knew the Hetwan females were illusions. And I knew that different species do different things to get by and stay alive. And there was the fact that the Hetwan females were flying bags of guts. Still, it wasn't something I needed to see. Not something I wanted imprinted on my memory.

After that it was a sort of orgy of creepy slaughter. The flying gut-bags flew lower and lower, teasing and flirting in a hideous ballet. More got caught and more were ripped apart, and more guts were eaten and spilled, and Dionysus and Jalil and I made it to the front of the wagon.

April and Ganymede jumped down to the ground, along with Jalil. They sliced the harnesses of the horses. Ganymede and April grabbed the reins. David was standing around with nothing to do but look tough and I had this fleeting moment of hope that maybe, maybe it would all be easy.

Then some of the Hetwan began howling a whole new noise.

"They know they have been tricked," Ganymede observed.

"How do they know?"

"They should be birthing by now. Small Hetwan should be forming around their waists. It is their way."

A handful of the Hetwan suddenly shot us some sharp looks. The ones who were still busy enjoying the illusion, so to speak, were unfazed. But this few were done. They were wondering where the little Hetwan were. And they had suspicions.

With a buzz of wings and rush of slidey-glideys, they were after us.

David leaped down, chopped one down while still in midleap, landed, rolled, almost stabbed himself in the thigh with his sword, and jumped up again.

"Get on the damn horses!" he yelled.

April hauled the largest horse over. It was neighing and cavorting and not happy. Ganymede grabbed it, April grabbed it, Jalil grabbed it, and the horse was whinnying like it was about to be taken to the Friskies factory. The three of them by sheer brute force held the horse still while I tried to give a hand up to Dionysus.

"He's never gonna sit on it," I grunted. "Dionysus, just lie across its back."

David cut down another Hetwan. And now the more in-control Hetwan were beginning to see they had a problem. Fortunately, only about a third of the bugs carried the squirter attachments. Maybe some kind of specialization, I didn't know. All I knew was I was heaving the three-hundred-pound god of good times onto a horse that didn't want to carry him and my back was straining and the veins were popping in my neck.

David slashed. The Hetwan were arming. More were pulling away from the gut-bags. It was going bad real fast now. It was going really bad.

Then the weight was off my hands. Dionysus was on the horse. I swear I heard the horse say something R-rated as he took the weight. April was being lifted up onto a much luckier horse by Ganymede. And two unsquirtered Hetwan were closing in on me.

I had nothing. No weapon. So I stepped in, closed up the distance, and swung a hard right uppercut. Two of the three mouth parts snapped. I followed with a left jab that collapsed the Hetwan's face like a Mylar balloon that's been popped.

I heard the spit.

I turned and saw David take the venom on his left forearm. A round patch burned like a match head.

David bellowed. He swung his sword in a downward arc and the Hetwan fell in two pieces.

Now the Hetwan orgy was definitely over. They came at us in a mass. I don't know how many, maybe thirty, at least ten of them already armed with their venomous tips.

And throughout all this, the party on the platform raged on. That was Dionysus for you. The stupid old fart, the drunken idiot, the immortal jackass was still throwing a party, even as his horse staggered away into the trees.

Then, a very sudden change in my perspective.

The nymphs, the satyrs, the happy party-goers, male and female, all spilled from the platform and went for the Hetwan.

Not to hurt them. No, they were just going to show the bugs how to party.

Dionysus had realized what I had not: The Hetwan knew the gut-bags were illusions, but it hadn't occurred to them that the rest of the party was as well.

It was the bimbo/himbo cavalry to the rescue. They rushed to surround the Hetwan, kissing, grabbing, stroking, giggling, offering drinks, offering pretty much whatever.

And the Hetwan didn't get it. They started attacking the party. They fired their venom. Fabulous babes cried in annoyance. Not pain, I guess that wasn't in old Dionysus's repertoire. But he could imagine up some pretty good petulance.

With the result that a whole corps of Pamela Anderson Lees and Leonardo DiCaprios were being nailed with burning venom and crying, "Oh, not like that, lover!" and, "Didn't your mother ever teach you how to treat a lady?" and, "Ah, so you like it rough, eh?"

Dionysus was clop-clopping away on his pissed-off horse, with April right behind him. Jalil and Ganymede were sharing a horse. David and I ended up horseless, running like hell after them.

We ran till we couldn't run anymore. The horses led us around the drop-offs, at least. That helped. We made good time, I guess; it was impossible to tell. It felt like we were running a long way.

A pair of flying Hetwan spotted us after half an hour, but they made the stupid move of trying to take us on alone, and only one had a squirter. We killed them both.

After that we had to flop and rest. The three horses were bushed. So were those of us on foot.

"I think we have made good our escape," Dionysus announced. "Let us share a celebratory drink!" And a barrel of vino appeared out of nowhere. Ganymede got ready to tap the barrel.

David strode over, stiff-legged and mad, raised

his sword, and smashed it down on the barrel. Red wine gushed from the burst staves.

"We haven't escaped, you clown!" David yelled. "You think the Hetwan are just going to go off peaceably and tell Ka Anor they lost his lunch?"

Dionysus looked shocked. Ganymede made a pretty frown.

"There's no harm in a drink," Dionysus protested.

I said, "You know, I like a drink as well as the next guy, but this probably isn't the time."

"We are deep in Hetwan territory," Jalil agreed. "They can fly. They can evidently see well in the dark. There are a lot of them. On our side we have four kids, two gods, one sword, and a pocketknife."

"Two gods whose powers are to throw a really great party," I grumbled. "Don't get me wrong: Any other time, man, you two are my gods. But a god of war would come in handy right about now."

"You wouldn't like Ares," Ganymede said. "He's very temperamental."

"Yeah, or maybe he just doesn't like fairies," I said. Ganymede frowned as if what I'd said made no sense, but he was going to be polite and let it pass.

"Ten-minute rest, and then we move," David said. "At right angles to our present line, to throw them off. Then we'll head straight toward . . ." He stopped and scowled at the gods. "Where are we going, anyway? Christopher says you two can lead us out of Hetwan territory."

"Assuredly," Dionysus said. "We can lead you to Olympus itself. We'll all be safe there, and oh, what a party we'll have! No one can revel like my fellow Olympians."

"Except for Ares," Ganymede added helpfully. "He's very tense."

"Yeah, whatever," David said, sounding very tense. "Which way is Olympus?"

"There's a sentence you never thought you'd be saying," April remarked.

"Olympus is . . . " Dionysus looked around at the softly cooing woods. Then he pointed. "That way."

"That's the direction you were heading," Jalil pointed out, making an effort to keep his tone of voice ever so reasonable. "That's toward Ka Anor."

"Yes, of course. Ganymede and I were far from home. We were on a mission, you see. It is harvest time in Fairy Land. I have always officiated at the annual grape harvest. The fairies are very respectful of Olympus. And the fairy women, well . . ." He leered. Of course he pretty much always leered.

"You guys were on your way to Fairy Land?" April said.

"And of course we know why Ganymede was heading there," I said brightly.

Ganymede evidently didn't get the joke, or else didn't care. "I separated from Dionysus to visit a friend I have not seen in a long time. The Hetwan captured me first. Only later was I reunited with Dionysus, who had been captured at the border of Fairy Land. It was a surprise because we had passed through all the Hetwan lands, including the great city of Ka Anor, and been unmolested."

"Wait a minute," David said. "Wait a minute. Are you telling me the way to Olympus is through Ka Anor's territory?"

"Yes, indeed. It is so," Dionysus said. "Now, would you like a drink?"

"Several," I said.

"Man, you've got to be kidding," Jalil said. "To save these two we have to pass through Ka Anor's hometown?"

"Through his palace, in a sense," Ganymede said. "The Hetwan have apparently decided to break the treaty with Zeus. We must be at war. Otherwise they would not have seized the two of us."

"Let's get going," David said sourly. "We've sat here too long. The Hetwan have to figure we'll head back to Fairy Land. They can't know that the four of us are screwed there. The last thing they'll figure is that we'll head straight toward Ka Anor."

"Yes, that will surprise them," Jalil said dryly. "Self-destructive tendencies are always a surprise."

"How the hell do we pass as bugs?" I demanded. "Are you people all crazy? Ka Anor's town? It'll be nothing but Ally McBugs and gutbags. Which are we supposed to be? You don't think maybe we'll stand out? We'll be the only people with eyes *inside* our heads."

Ganymede said, "You are mistaken, Christopher. The great city of Ka Anor is filled with many peoples and nationalities. Many mortals pass through on business of one type or another. The Hetwan purchase goods from abroad. And they are greatly interested in books, marvels, and machines."

"Are they?" Jalil perked up.

"Yeah, great, now Jalil wants to be a Hetwan."

"It may give us a way to trick them," he said. "We have a marvel: the CD player."

"Well, then, hi-ho, hi-freaking-ho, it's off to Ka Anor we go," I said. "I'm just disappointed good old Senna can't be here with us. But she always manages to miss out on the real fun, doesn't she?"

We marched as David had suggested, at right angles to our last movement. Or as much at an angle as you can go when your path is strewn with monstrous potholes and giant ice-cream sundaes. Not to mention singing trees.

After two hours, during which we may have covered anywhere from three miles to twelve feet of actual straight-line movement, we headed toward Olympus.

Worried? Nah. I was going to be immortal. If I lived that long.

Chapter XV

We walked through the night. Probably in circles. Dionysus had one horse, we'd managed to lose one, and we traded off on the other one.

We were having dark thoughts, the four of us. At least I was. Jalil was muttering to himself. David was trying to look bold and filled with purpose, but the burn wound was hurting him bad. It wasn't life threatening, it wasn't going to drag him down, but it must have hurt like hell.

Ganymede remained quiet and a little withdrawn, despite April's occasional efforts to engage him in conversation. I don't know what the girl was thinking. Zeus may have swung both ways, but Ganymede didn't even cop cheap down-the-shirt glances or anything. April had no effect on him, and frankly, I was beginning to resent her for trying so hard. What, humans weren't good enough? She had to have some long-legged, lean, muscular, sweet-natured, incredibly handsome, barely dressed stud-muffin?

I mean, yeah, guys think that way. But I expected more of April. Whatever happened to the idea of women caring more about sense of humor and inner beauty? Ganymede had no sense of humor at all. Unlike, say, me.

Dionysus was a monumental butt pain. Party boys are fun at parties, but the party was suspended for the moment. Party all gone, serious stuff to deal with, and every other word from his mouth was, "Shall we not have wenches? Should we not imbibe of the sacred vine?"

And he wasn't the fastest-moving god I've ever seen. He wanted to stop for a rest every few minutes, despite hogging the poor horse. Not to mention his annoying and tempting habit of causing barrels of wine and kegs of beer to appear out of nowhere.

But he told stories. Not great stories, but they filled the hours.

"Zeus, a great god, a good fellow, I love him like a father. He is my father, of course, but you know what I mean. But as great a god as he is, he cannot hold his mead. It's some strange quality of mead, I suppose, because he is very able to restrain his baser impulses when drinking wine or ale. But you pour a few barrels of mead in him and look out! Ha-ha! Many's the maidenly shepherd girl who was tending her flock in the foothills of Olympus, only to have Zeus appear disguised as a bull or a ram, drunk and randy, and ha! That's the truth of Heracles's birth: Zeus was reeling, roaring drunk on mead.

"Anyway, there was this particular day, I remember it well, we'd all been enjoying the fruits of the vine, and Zeus got into the mead. I said to him, 'Zeus, Father, you know how you get when you drink mead.' Artemis, who is a terrible prude, you know, said, 'Half the maidens between here and Troy know how he gets when he drinks mead.' So Zeus says, 'Only half? Pour me a tall one, Ganymede, I have work to do!' "

April stopped throwing herself at Ganymede long enough to say, "I can't imagine why people stopped worshiping you people."

Dionysus missed the sarcasm. "Who has stopped worshiping us?"

"Everyone in the old world," April said a little harshly.

"But of course they have, young woman. We left, didn't we? We came to Everworld. How can you expect people to worship a god they can't see from time to time?"

"Yeah, April," Jalil prodded, failing to suppress a smirk. "How can you?"

"It's getting quiet," David observed. "The trees."

"Yes, I think the landscape is changing," Jalil said. "Fewer detours, able to move in a straighter line. The trees are thinning out. Fewer scoops."

"Man, when does the sun come up around here?" I asked.

"I don't know, but I think maybe we need to grab some sleep, wait for the sun to come up, and see what we're looking at before we go any farther," David said.

"Well, if you say so, General Lee." I dropped the food sacks and then dropped my body onto the ground. "Another night on the ground. Great. I'm getting used to it, that's what's so sad."

"Ah, but I can provide some comforts," Dionysus offered.

"Too whipped to party," I said through a yawn.

"Surely, this is not the time for revelry," Dionysus said, sounding doubtful, as though he'd never before spoken those words and they didn't sound quite right. "I am no god of sleep, but I can make sleep easier."

And then, in the midst of bleak emptiness, mounds of silk pillows were stacked on what looked like Persian rugs.

Dionysus looked over his handiwork and winced. "The scene of an orgy, but with neither nubile maidens nor randy satyrs. It seems empty."

I lay back against a bolster the size of a beanbag chair and pulled another pillow down on top of me. It was all in my head, all an illusion. But it felt soft and warm and inviting.

I was asleep in seconds. And the beauty of it was that I was asleep in the real world, too.

My real-world subconscious felt the addition of new experience, felt the dream-woven images of Hetwan venom and gut-bags and wood chippers. Through my dim, powered-down brain floated images of David's arm burning, and Dionysus laughing, and Ganymede.

My dreams were like a river joined by a stream. Their color and temperature were changed, the flow disturbed. I saw myself at work, stacking the pages into the feed, watching the brilliant lights of the Xerox machine glow and darken, glow and darken.

I was making copies.

Late at night, after the store had closed its doors. My boss was there, drinking beer with two other guys, their faces lit by the glow of a computer monitor.

Copying. Copying something wrong.

Not my problem. Not my business. People

could copy whatever they wanted, as long as it wasn't copyrighted.

But these copies weren't from customers. These were pages downloaded off the Web, printed out, then copied in large numbers.

Wrong.

The symbol there, there on the page, that twisted cross, wrong.

All a dream. Nothing more. A dream inside a dream.

And my sleeping mind slipped away to other wispy thoughts and images.

CHAPTER XVI

I dreamed of April. She was floating above me, loose robe flowing on a breeze. I smiled. Her robe stiffened, extended, buzzed, she dropped.

"Ahh!"

The Hetwan landed on me. Mouth parts chewed the air in front of my face.

I shoved, a panic shove, but enough. The Hetwan didn't weigh much. Like throwing off a ten-year-old.

I rolled, yelled, "Hetwan!"

But everyone was already awake, all yelling, all flailing and punching and kicking. David was hacking through the aliens, working Galahad's reborn sword.

Twenty of them. They had attacked from the air. April's hair tangled a Hetwan's mouth parts. Ganymede landed a nice kick that crumpled one of the creatures. Dionysus was swatting with his big beefy hands, no concept of fighting.

I kicked my way free. Saw one of the horses rearing, whinnying in terror, saw his rope snap, and he was just haunches thundering away.

Weapons. We needed weapons.

Two Hetwan jump-flew at me. They hit me from opposite sides, knocked the air from my chest, I fell to my knees, staggered, sucking, unable to draw breath.

They were chewing at me, chewing, I felt flesh tear, saw my own blood, sucked a quart of oxygen, slammed a shoulder into the mouth, slammed the other direction, tripped. On me. More now. On me. Face in the dirt, fingers grabbing grass, pulling myself along, a stick!

A branch. Crooked, too heavy, but better than fingernails. I swung the branch back in an awkward jerk that grazed one of the bugs.

Suddenly I broke free. I couldn't make it to my feet, ran squatted down, felt a burn, a terrible burn, just a graze along my shoulder, but the pain was electric.

Fury boiled up. I turned, whipped the branch around. It had two side branches, kept me from using it very well.

"Jalil!" I yelled.

He was close by. He had his knife out. Saw

what I wanted. He whipped the blade down, sliced off one branch, whipped it up, removed the other, and something I hadn't thought about, chopped the top of the main stick off at an angle.

Now I had a four-foot staff, a bit crooked, but with a dull point.

I didn't waste any time. I stabbed a Hetwan in his belly. The point didn't go in, but the alien went down. I clubbed another of them, and suddenly the Hetwan withdrew.

I heard the trees moaning. Wood chippers? Some other horror?

The Hetwan backed off, disappeared in the darkness.

"Are they giving up?" April panted.

David said, "No. Something they have to deal with. I don't know what's going on, but they'll be back. That way. Run!"

"We are very near to Ka Anor's city," Dionysus said, and if I'd had a clear head, I'd probably have heard the warning in his voice.

But I was too busy running. All of us, thundering along, no food bags, no horses, no nothing but sheer adrenaline.

I ran. Stopped. Stopped very suddenly because the earth just ended.

But momentum had carried me, a second too long, a second earlier, if only I'd seen and now,

now I was waving my arms, windmilling, trying to step back but overbalanced. One foot out on space, oh, God, I was Wile E. Coyote.

I was going to fall.

I heaved the stick away, forward, hoping that whole equal-and-opposite-reaction thing would work.

A hand landed on my shoulder. April held me, pulled me slowly back. I was on land. On land. Both feet planted.

My knees buckled. I hit the dirt, fell forward onto my elbows, and just breathed for a while.

"What are you doing, Christo — oh, wow." Jalil.

He stepped past me, almost to the edge, then stepped back. The others arrived, David and Ganymede and Dionysus. I stood up on rubber legs.

"Thanks, want to get married?" I said to April. She'd saved my life. But I'd saved hers before. Fair trade.

"I fear the fall would have killed you," Ganymede said.

"I fear it would have killed me about nine times over," I said.

We were standing on the edge of the granddaddy of all the little scoops we'd seen. It was like a moon crater.

If I had fallen off the edge of the chasm, I'd have dropped maybe five hundred feet straight down before the slope came out to meet me. Fifty stories. Five times the big drop on a roller coaster. Then I'd have slid or tumbled or rolled or cart-wheeled another two, three thousand feet maybe. That's several Sears Towers stacked up.

Of course I'd have been little more than a chunky liquid by that point.

Gradually the angle extended so as I reached the bottom I'd have been rolling more horizontally and less vertically. But this fact would probably have been lost on me since I'd have been both dead and dismembered and dead all over again.

Glass daggers reached up and out. That's how they looked, anyway. Like black and brown and rust-red and milky-white glass. Only not smooth glass. Shattered, broken glass. It looked like some-one had dug a hole using a nuclear bomb, and then laser-blasted the hole till the dirt and sand had turned to glass. And then had left it to be cracked and shattered by the ravages of earth-quakes till there were ridges of jet glass stalagmites, and gullies of creamy glass spears, and Mars-scapes of red glass razors.

A person falling down into this monstrous hole would be raw hamburger.

The glass crater extended maybe five miles from rim to rim. It was impossible to guess distance accurately. Nothing in this vista made sense. There was nothing to hold up and use as a measuring stick.

From the center of the crater rose what I guess could be called a tower. Or a city. Or the hypodermic needle a junkie sees in his nightmares. It was, conservatively, a mile across at its base. Probably more.

It rose at an angle that mirrored the crater walls, only more acute still. The tower, the city, whatever it was, seemed to have been squeezed up out of the bedrock. It was living rock the color of dried blood.

It rose, uneven, imperfect, but roughly symmetrical, till it was nearly as tall as the crater walls. Then it was like someone had taken a huge knife and cut the top off like a French-cut green bean. This part, the angled cut, was hollow, open to the stars and the moon and the sun and looking like it could swallow up any of the above.

It was a vast, fat-bottomed, hypodermic needle.

"It's the stingers," April said. "Look, it's like the Hetwan's stingers."

She was right. It looked like the model for the Hetwan SuperSoakers. Only larger. Larger in the same way that Mount Everest is larger than what you made at the beach with your little plastic pail.

The needle extended till its very top, its point, was level with us. A person standing atop that point could have peeked beyond the crater, could have looked around at the surrounding countryside.

A glow came from inside the needle tip. A green glow that slowly faded from bright to dark and back to bright.

Something was alive inside that needle. I had a pretty good idea what or who.

And many somethings were alive on the outside of the needle. There was a sort of Pueblo thing going on, whatever those Indians are called who built mud houses in the sides of cliffs.

It was a city, with twinkly lights and buildings and, for all I knew, a Gap, a Starbucks, and a Mickey D's on every corner.

Around the base of the needle, in the flatlands between the petering out of the crater slope and the start of the needle slope, was a ring of long, curved lakes. They each seemed to be about two football fields in length, shaped like long kidney beans, and they were arranged so they never touched, but overlapped one another. You could walk through this belt of lakes, but not without doubling back and forth at least twice.

And no one was going to be taking the old bass boat out for a day on any of those lakes. They appeared, at first glance at least, to be filled with lava.

"Ah," Dionysus wheezed as he grabbed me for support. "The city of Ka Anor. Shall we have a drink to celebrate?"

I didn't want to get hysterical. I wanted to remain calm. So I considered my words carefully, and just as I was about to explode, David beat me to it.

"You stupid, drunken, senile son of a —— !" he roared. "This is where you lead us? To this?"

Dionysus looked mildly surprised. "But you knew we had to pass through the city of Ka Anor."

David looked like his head was going to explode. Normally I'd have enjoyed that.

"You didn't tell us it was like this. You didn't tell us it was five miles of broken glass and lava lakes and some kind of mile-high termite mound. What are we . . . What the hell are . . ." He jabbed his finger impotently at the sight below us. "What do you think we're going to do? Walk across that?"

"Ah, I see your problem," Dionysus allowed. "One doesn't walk to the city of Ka Anor, dear boy, one flies."

"One what?"

"One flies," the old fool said, laughing as though it were obvious.

"One doesn't have any damned wings, does one?" I yelled.

David was simply staring now, and he looked like he was torn between a desire to laugh till he cried and a desire to cry till he found a rope and hung himself.

"Ah, but the Hetwan have wings, and so do the creatures they call Red Wings," Dionysus said. "The Red Wings fly into and out of the city. And they carry guests as well. Four of the brutes carried me through on my last visit. It lacks a certain dignity, but it serves."

The four of us, the sane ones, the mortals, the nonlunatics, were left speechless. I'm never speechless. But the enormity of his madness was too great to swallow in one bite.

I decided the only way to begin to cope with this was to ignore the two gods entirely.

"We'd have a better chance of walking through Hel's Underworld than to get through there. Or across there. Or, whatever, because I can't even figure out the right word for what we'd have to do."

"Not only could we not make it across, we couldn't make it down this slope," Jalil said.

"We couldn't make it six feet. The U.S. Marines couldn't make it six feet."

David nodded agreement, but the general was already looking ahead. "Yeah, but if you had artillery you could sit up here and blow the hell out of everything. This is an amazing defense, amazing fort or whatever, but if you had artillery —" He broke off and nodded to himself, satisfied.

April put her hand gently on David's arm. "David, I'm pretty sure we don't have any artillery."

"Yeah, and then if we just had the right Pokémon we'd be all set. David, why don't you go stand with the other two fantasy figures while April and Jalil and I stay here in reality and try to figure out what to do?"

"Not much to decide," David said, unfazed by my snottiness. "We can't go around. It's too far. And the odds of us not being caught are too great. So we're going through. Which means doing what Dionysus said."

"You're on his side now?" I said in a low shriek.

Jalil said, "Dionysus, are the Red Wings Hetwan? I mean, do they talk? Do they communicate? Are they sentient?"

The world's oldest party animal thought that over, his hand twitching involuntarily for a glass.

"I don't know, exactly. It's so hard to tell the difference between mere mortals and mere animals."

"What with us all being equally 'mere,'" April added, shooting an annoyed look at Ganymede.

Ganymede said, "They don't look as the Hetwan look. They have wings, but different in form. I did not remark that they spoke."

Jalil said, "Look, the Hetwan are aliens, but they're not Martians or whatever. They aren't some technologically advanced race. They didn't get here on spaceships. They don't have communicators. Or even phones. So how do our Hetwan tell other Hetwan we're coming this way? They don't. Not until they see them, face-to-face. So maybe, even probably, the Hetwan in the city don't know to be on the lookout for us. Right? They know to be looking for Dionysus or Ganymede, maybe, but not us. Not some scruffy old humans."

I resisted the urge to scream. Now Jalil was in this, too. "Hey, they've seen these two before. They know what they look like. They're gonna know that Ka Anor is hungry."

"That may help us, actually," April said thoughtfully. "I mean, look, these two aren't carrying any other clothes, right? So most likely the toga and the loincloth thing are like uniforms, right? Ganymede, do you ever wear anything besides a loincloth?"

The god of fabulous shook his head and looked a little perturbed. I don't think the idea had ever occurred to him. And I think, as the idea percolated through his head, that he kind of liked the notion.

"Okay, so the Hetwan and everyone see a portly gentleman in a toga, they know it's Dionysus. But a portly gentleman in something else? Maybe not. I think we need a quick makeover. We trade clothes."

"Then we find some Red Wings, move so fast the word never catches up to us," David said, making his "I'm now satisfied with my grand plan" look.

We were wearing a motley assortment of the dirty stuff we'd shown up in, plus the various shifts, shirts, tunics, skins, and rags we'd acquired along the way.

I looked at my clothes. At the clothes of the gods. At least theirs were clean.

"I call the toga," I said.

Twenty minutes later I was wrapped about three times around with a toga that could have been used as a sail. Jalil had inherited the loincloth.

He wasn't happy about it. But we wanted whoever was wearing the immortal loincloth to look as unlike Ganymede as possible. I was more Ganymede's build, Jalil was more his height. But there was no escaping the fact that not even an Ally McBug would ever confuse Jalil with Ganymede.

Dionysus was squeezed into my clothes with a few contributions from David. It was sad to see. Togas are kind to the hefty. T-shirts and jeans are not. Dionysus looked like the street person who was last in line at the Salvation Army thrift shop.

Ganymede wore my jeans like a second skin. They were about four inches short and would, had they not been genuine Levi's, have blown apart from the strain. He wore a shirt, open because there was no way to button it. And here's the kicker: He still looked good.

Not the case with Jalil.

"You look like a Slim Jim wearing Pampers," I said.

Jalil had no comeback. I wasn't even exaggerating, and he knew it. He had wound the loincloth as tight as it would go, but whatever magic force kept the garment hanging precariously on Ganymede's Nicole Kidman butt, the same magic didn't work for Jalil. He had to yank the thing up onto his doorknob hip bones every few seconds.

"You look great," April lied gamely. Then she laughed.

"Thanks, April," Jalil said. "There's nothing like a woman's derisive ridicule to make a man feel good."

"Okay, let's go," David said.

We set off around the rim of the crater. Sheer destruction to our right, tight woods to our left. Hetwan might appear from the woods at any moment. All they'd have to do is yell, "Boo!" real loud and we'd fall off the cliff and have ten, twenty seconds to scream our throats bloody before we hit the Cuisinart.

"See, this is why movies and TV are so much

better than real life," I said. "Doesn't matter what movie. Even some lame straight-to-cable, Dolph Lundgren piece of crap, if there's fighting going on, everyone has cool clothes. I mean, it's a given. Could be your Armani suit, could be your cool leather jacket, maybe your tank top, maybe your Mad Max gear, doesn't matter. Keanu in *The Matrix*? Always in some cool, full-length leather coat or whatever."

"Yeah, great outfit for hand-to-hand combat," Jalil said sarcastically. "Full-length coat. Good idea. Ever try to even move wearing something like that? Let alone kung fu?"

"You'd trade it in a heartbeat for that loin-cloth," I said.

"Got that right."

We walked along like mountain goats with a death wish for more than an hour. It was warming up as the sun rose in the sky. Not hot exactly, but humid.

Then the crater lip took a dip and all at once we were looking down at a platform cut back into the crater wall. It was a flat space, set thirty feet lower than the crater rim. Trees rimmed the top, and several sets of stone steps led down from tree level to what could only be a landing pad.

A dozen Red Wings rested there. No need to check in with Dionysus, these were clearly Red

Wings. As I watched, one of them unfolded his wings, spread them probably thirty feet, then folded them back. The wings were the color of strawberries. Definitely red.

The creature itself was no bigger than a Great Dane. It had a tiny head dominated by big bug eyes so that it evoked a huge dragonfly. But the wings were broad and triangular and leathery. Twin tentacles extended from the breast below the wings. At the moment they were curled up in tight spirals like a neatly stored garden hose.

The Red Wings sat on two fluffy-looking feet, or whatever. Anyway, where the feet should be, there were feathery fans, quite large. These, along with much of the body, were white.

"Strawberries and cream," April said. "They're kind of pretty. If you don't look at the eyes."

"How does something that small operate wings that big?" Jalil asked suspiciously. "It can't possibly have the muscles or the energy."

"Add that to your big list of stuff that can't be, but is," I said.

"Come," Dionysus said, feeling in charge for the moment. "I will give orders to these brutes."

He started down the steps with all of us trailing him close. Dionysus wasn't much of a god but in a weird place, trapped between terror on the one side and horror on the other, you tended to want to grab onto any god you had hanging around.

"Ho there!" Dionysus shouted to the Red Wings. "Lovely day, is it not? We require passage for six to the city yonder."

The Red Wings didn't look as if they cared, but nevertheless, they began to unfold their wings.

"Good fellows," Dionysus said.

The Red Wings powered up the fan-legs they sat on. They moved faster and faster, becoming a blur of what could conceivably be white feathers. You got the impression of propellers or helicopter rotors.

One by one they rose, hovering unsteadily above us. It was still impossible to believe those things could move wings that broad. I was seeing it and still not believing it.

Now old Dionysus was our tour guide. "Simply stand still and they will lift you up," he said. "Would anyone care for a bit of liquid refreshment?"

My hair was blowing in the breeze created by the large wings and the small fans. The Red Wing above me uncoiled its tentacles and began to wrap them down between my legs and beneath my armpits. I was facing the vast crater of broken glass, lava, and a gigantic stone hypodermic, and I said, "Damned straight, I'd like a drink."

A glass of wine materialized in Ganymede's

hand, he looked at me, smiled, and suddenly the glass was out of his hand and into mine.

This guy could bartend anywhere.

I took a deep drink of something nasty sweet. Mead, I believe. It's made with honey. Chick drink if ever there was one. But I didn't care because I was scared and I had pretty good reason to be scared.

I felt my feet come off the ground and for a moment I wasn't sure if it was the booze or the big bug. Then I looked down and there was no ground beneath my feet. Or at least what ground there was was a sheer drop down the face of the Hancock Building with everyone on every floor sticking swords out the window.

Five hundred feet not quite straight down. Five-hundred-foot wall of jagged glass shards. And what was stupid was the fact that I was even worrying about the glass shards, because a five-hundred-foot drop will kill you way dead even if the bottom was lined with pillows.

I finished my glass and grabbed onto the cable-thick tentacles and hoped the big red bug hadn't gotten the word that I was a bad guy.

I tried to focus on the hypo tower. Like once we got there it'd be all fresh-baked muffins and hot chocolate. But you just can't ignore a five-hundred-foot drop. You just can't. You just cannot stop asking yourself intelligent questions like, "If he drops me, will I scream all the way down? Won't I have to breathe like six times and so start screaming six different times?" And, "Am I going to crap myself and actually have time to contemplate that fact while I fall?" And, "Won't there be a few seconds of unbearable agony before I die, or can I at least just die right away?"

I looked back, back toward the cliff wall, which seemed like it was a very long way away. April and Ganymede and Jalil and David and Dionysus were strung out behind me, hovering, wobbling, looking like they were going to blow chunks that wouldn't hit ground till tomorrow.

Dionysus was being carried by two of the big red bugs. Typical of him to lie earlier about needing four bugs. Or maybe the extra bugs had been an honor, what with him being a god.

I could picture it: The bugs had orders to fly us out over the deepest part of the crater, then drop us. They were toying with us. It was all some sick Hetwan mind game.

Then, back at the platform that now seemed like heaven to me, I saw the Hetwan, our Hetwan, the brothers of all those we'd smoked thus far, surge out of the woods. They assembled there and gaped at us. Some of them, anyway. There were fewer. Maybe the others were off looking for us in the woods.

"David!" I yelled.

He twisted around to look back. I'd only thought I was afraid. Now I was really afraid. Sick afraid. Muscles-turning-to-water afraid. Uncontrollable-trembling, little-moaning-noises, screaming-in-your-head afraid.

Imagine having to walk a tightrope stretched above an active volcano. That's bad. Now imagine someone is shooting at you. That's when you dip into the secret reserve pouch of adrenaline.

The Hetwan unfolded their wings. They flapped, dropped gracefully off the side of the crater, and swooped toward us.

"Faster! Faster!" I screamed at the big red bug. Like that was going to work, like the bug was anything but a bug, and me yelling like a baboon who's spotted a leopard.

I felt the tug of the tentacles as they tightened. Oh, my God, they were going to choke me, squeeze the life out of me, do an anaconda. Oh, God, oh God.

No, wait. We were going faster!

My brain was busy being terrified, so like a

computer multitasking, it slowed down the processing of this new realization. I could almost watch the thought moving along a slow, slow conveyor belt like a box of Wheaties at the grocery store.

Then, "David! Jalil! April! The bugs! You can talk to them!" I was screaming, and man, if I'd heard me I'd have been pretty sure I'd popped a few rivets.

But then, there was David yelling, "Turn back, turn back toward them," up at his Red Wing. And damned if the crazy boy wasn't heading back toward the Hetwan.

April yelled, "David, are you insane?"

"If the Hetwan get to the city we're screwed. They'll tell everyone who we are. What we've done. They have to die."

It was flat-out the weirdest thing I've ever seen. David whipping out his sword while hanging in the tentacles of a big red bug and playing Snoopy and the Red Baron with Hetwan high above a landscape that made the inside of a whirring garbage disposal look comfy.

The boy is crazy. The boy is Senna's tool. The boy is a humorless jerk a lot of the time. But the boy has radioactive, titanium *cojones*.

"He's right," I heard myself saying. To which

another part of me, the sensible part said, "He's right? He's nuts!"

And then, to my eternal horror, I heard myself yell, "Turn back, big red bug. Back toward the Hetwan."

It did occur to me that I had no weapon. That did occur to me. But David was right: The Hetwan had to die before they could rat us out to Ka Anor.

David aimed his big red bug on an intercept course. I followed David. I passed Jalil, hanging there like me, only wearing an oversized diaper. My bug passed his and I yelled, "Come on, man, you want to live forever?"

"No. But eighty or ninety years would be nice," he said. But then I heard him yelling and turning his bug around to come after me. April was turning as well, more in solidarity than anything else. I mean, at least I could try and hit one of the Hetwan; what was April going to do?

Dionysus, big shock, was not joining the fight.

"Hey, Lord of the Dance, let's go!" I yelled.

"You can at least dazzle them with some more gut-bags."

Ganymede was a different story. He was dressed like Jethro from the *Beverly Hillbillies*, hanging there from bug tentacles like the rest of us, but he was going to get in the game. I was scared in more dimensions than I knew existed, I was desperate, I was screwed, I was toast, I was going to my own death, and as far as I was concerned right at that moment anyone, anyone, anyone who wanted to go into battle at my side was welcome. Gay? Chick? Come on down, boys, girls. If you're getting between me and the bad guys it's all good.

The Hetwan were lower than we were by maybe ten feet. That is, ten feet below our swinging, hanging bodies. And they looked like they were slower than the Red Wings. Not that the Wings were exactly F-16's. The Red Wings made maybe six miles an hour, running speed, the Hetwan three or four, a fast walking pace. So we were coming together at probably ten miles an hour, which was both agonizingly slow and startlingly fast, depending on which panicked fragment of my brain was doing the thinking.

The Hetwan saw us. David trimmed his sails like the sailor he is, barking out manly, peremptory commands as if he were on detached duty from the Royal Navy circa 1812.

"Left five degrees! Take her down three feet!"

The Red Wings obeyed. Now, why did they obey? Why did they understand English? How is it they knew what a foot was — weren't they at least on metric?

W.T.E.

David and the lead of what I now counted as nine Hetwan were closing in fast. The lead Hetwan was screwing his SuperSoaker on. David was limbering up his sword shoulder.

I heard Jalil yell, "You can swing."

It struck me as completely idiotic, till he added, "Pendulum. You can swing back and forth."

I twisted my head around, and sure enough, Jalil was picking up momentum, swinging left and right, back and forth like the clock in an entomologist's nightmare.

I kicked my legs, trying to mimic Jalil's movements. But I decided forward and back would be a better plan. I kicked my legs out and pulled them back, causing fairly severe crotch pain. I picked up some momentum. It was grade school all over again, me on the swing, yelling, "I'm gonna go so high I go right over the top, ha-ha."

Long swing forward. Long swing back.

David and the lead Hetwan closed at the slow/fast pace of ten m.p.h. The Hetwan spit. David swung ponderously out of the way. He waited for the swing to carry him back, swung, and missed.

The Hetwan drifted by him, turned with all the agility and grace of a 747, and came back around after him.

One thing was obvious, and welcome: The Hetwan were not dogfighters. The sky was not where they battled.

A second Hetwan was on an intercept course for me. He had a stinger, which pissed me off, it wasn't fair. I was unarmed. I had nothing. I had my fists, which weren't going to be George Foremans with my shoulders yanked upward by the supporting tentacles.

Then, an idea. An insight. A flash of sheer desperation.

Toga.

I started yanking frantically at the fabric, yanking, yanking like a guy wrapped in his bedsheets trying to find the cigarette butt he dropped.

I yanked. I hurt. But, man, it was all I had. The cloth was bunched up through my crotch. No way to get it clear.

"Jalil! Throw me your knife!"

"No way, you'll drop it."

I swung far back, almost intercepting the angle of Jalil's side-to-side swing.

A Hetwan spit at David, missed. David twisted, tried to get at the flying monkey but couldn't get a shot. It was *Top Gun* with everyone switching to herbal tea. It was the Battle of Britain with the parts of the Luftwaffe and the Royal Air Force being played by butterflies.

"I need to cut this thing," I cried.

"Use your teeth," April shouted.

"Oh." I yanked a fold of cloth up to my mouth and, I swear, chewed a bite out of it. With a start made, I ripped. Ripped and yanked, and my bug was coming within venom range, no time left. He spit.

I caught the flame on a fold of toga wrapped around my left forearm. It burned, then died out, leaving behind a blackened hole.

Ahead, David swung again and missed again, and now we were in the thick of the Hetwan. I heard Jalil bellow in pain. He was beating frantically at one leg with the other. Flashed on Ganymede speeding toward his own foe. Saw April lift her legs, getting ready to kick. Yeah, that'd work. Kicking while hanging from a string.

I had my toga mostly free. *Rip*. *Rip*. Bunch. *Rip*. Enough remained for modesty, of which I had zero at the moment. My Hetwan was closing in, spit! I swung toward him, closing the distance, the spit, the venom, I could see it, a round ball of fire like a slow bullet.

My swing lifted me, I yanked up my legs, cleared the venom, reached the end of my arc just even with the Hetwan, whipped my toga out like a bullfighter working his cape. The toga caught breeze, opened, billowed, and enveloped the Hetwan.

The Hetwan's wings collapsed and he began to fall. He fell head down, the wind holding the toga over his head, defeating his limp-armed efforts to free himself. He was a Halloween ghost on his way to digging a hole in the field of red-black glass beneath us.

Just then David busted a move. He swung up, bounced, caught the bungee on the yank, flipped sneaks above, head below, and hacked at a passing Hetwan.

The Hetwan dropped.

"Yeah!" he yelled. "Die."

And I yelled it, too. We were getting that crazy, foaming-at-the-mouth, "I'll kill you!" rage going.

Two for our side. Then, something we hadn't considered.

A Hetwan aimed right at David's big red bug. He fired. The venom hit the Red Wing in one of his eyes. The first thing we'd heard from the Red

Wings was a screech like a chain saw hitting a nail.

David's bug lost it. He zoomed away at twice the speed we'd seen, zoomed away, with David yelling impotently. He was out of the fight.

Two for us. One for them. They still had us, seven to five. And we'd lost our only serious weapon.

Hetwan were all around us now; they seemed so much more numerous up close, like we were flying through a flock of them.

I'd played my one card, the old toga-in-the-face trick. Now I was just one big dumb white boy in a rag. I had nothing. David was out of it. And if David couldn't do much damage with a three-foot-long sword, I didn't see how Jalil was going to lay much hurting on the Hetwan with his pocketknife.

All I had was blunt force trauma. I swung way back, way forward. Impossible to time it, of course, all I could do was swing wildly and hope some Hetwan misjudged distance.

The creepy thing about the Hetwan was that the ones that didn't carry the SuperSoakers were still grabbing at the air with their mouth parts. I don't know what they thought they were going to eat. Maybe us.

I ripped a small shred of cloth, waited till I was

close, threw it in the face of an unarmed Hetwan. But he missed grabbing it. So much for hoping they'd choke.

Sudden agony. A venom ball in, just off my spine. I slapped frantically over my shoulder, couldn't reach it, screamed for help, senseless, no one could help, but the pain snatched my breath, terrified me.

I felt like the fire was burning right into me, burning through skin and through muscle into bone. Like it would eat its way all the way through and emerge, a burning, erupting pustule in my chest.

I started to cry. Nothing else to do, man, I was helpless. I was going to be burned alive, bit by bit. I kicked in frustration at a passing Hetwan, but was nowhere close to him.

My Red Wing turned back toward the city of Ka Anor, reverting to his original instructions, I guess. It brought me around to see April, scrabbling to drag her backpack around where she could get it.

And beyond her, Dionysus, hanging from his twin Red Wings, useless. He had a big goblet in one hand and was gulping red wine.

"Help us!" I yelled.

"I am," he cried. "I am powerless in this state."

He swallowed a half quart of the house Merlot

and his goblet refilled. It took me a second to track, what with being distracted by my own bitter weeping. Then I realized: He was sober. His powers came from the booze.

I barked out a shrill sobbing laugh. He was powerless till he was faced? Even then, what could he do? Distract everyone by throwing a midair costume ball?

"Ha!" April cried.

I twisted around. A spitwad flew past my face, missing my cheek by an inch. If I hadn't jerked around to see her I'd be breathing through my cheek.

April was hanging with a Hetwan hovering maybe three feet from her. It hovered like a malignant wasp looking to gather her pollen. I saw her toss a scattering of glitter at the Hetwan. The Hetwan was an unarmed one. His mouthparts worked frenziedly, snatching the glitter from the air. He was a seal and April was the trainer tossing sardines.

Only, what she was tossing was diamonds. Our diamonds. The ones the fairy had paid us for making him into MCI.

The Hetwan stuffed the diamonds in his face, and another Hetwan was zeroing toward her, anxious to join in.

Then I saw the Hetwan who was falling away

from April. The Hetwan who was writhing, tearing at his own thorax with his limp hands.

She was poisoning them! And they were going for it like goldfish who'd eat fish flakes till they blew up and died. They were helpless to resist!

Then a tremor, a chain-saw-on-steel shriek. I looked up. Saw the burn. Saw the fire eating into one of my supporting tendrils.

The tendril loosened, withdrew, sucked up into the Red Wing like a convenient retractable vacuum cleaner cord. The cord under my arms was gone. I slipped backward, arms waving, trying to hold my balance, fell over. Tried to clamp my legs, clamped, slipped, no! Fingers clawed air.

I fell.

I fell, head down, head down, all direction meaningless because all that mattered was down, oh, God, down!

My face was a scream. My mind was a scream. The ground, the shattered, twisted glass mountains so far below already reached up toward me, seemed to push up from the valley floor, anxious to touch me, to flay me, to shred me still alive.

I was going to fall forever. And for only a millisecond. Time stretched, time shrank, time meant nothing. I screamed, sucked in rushing air, screamed.

But I was still falling. Now time was time again. Worse still. Consciousness. Awareness. Reason. The knowing that I was falling, the understanding that I would die, and not yet, but so soon, and so inevitable.

The wind turned me, spinning. I was a propeller twirling down and down. The wind flipped me over and I was looking up. Far above, a sky filled with gut-bags swooping toward the Hetwan. David regaining control of his Red Wing and returning, sword at the ready. Diamond-poisoned Hetwan falling, writhing in pain as the hardest substance on Earth turned pulsing, squeezing digestive tracts into bleeding ribbons of flesh.

But all too late for me, as they became mere distant insects, no larger to me now than dragonflies. I was going to die. Dead already. Even now, any second, it would happen, any second, I couldn't even see, hurtling backward, rushing to impale myself on fields of broken bottles.

Dead. I was going to be dead. Maybe already was, for an angel floated into view, entered my field of vision, seemed to hover just above me, just out of reach, some dream no doubt, the mind's last desperate act of self-deception before the capital *T* Truth of mortality.

An arm. A hand. A look of concentration in lustrous eyes.

An angel. An angel dressed like Jethro Bodine.

Ganymede grabbed my left arm around the bicep. His hand went almost all the way around. I was a toy to him. I weighed nothing to a god.

He held me, drew me up toward him, almost to his face, almost as if he were going to kiss me and, boys and girls, he could have French-kissed me and taken me to see an ice-dancing competition, because I was one wretched, sobbing, snotting, diaper-wetting specimen of humanity right then.

"Rise!" Ganymede yelled up to his Red Wing.

But that was a case of easier said than done. Ganymede weighed at least two hundred fifty, and I was a good one-eighty myself, which made for four-hundred-plus pounds of hurtling, maximum-velocity load. The Red Wing had Ganymede, and Ganymede had me, but if we were slowing down I sure didn't see it.

I looked down, down between my feet, and saw doom. It was going to be a slope of black and dark blue glass, like some terrible mockery of a coral reef, with crusted arms of glass sticking out. We weren't going to die quickly. We'd hit extended shards that would rip the flesh an inch deeper with every ten feet we fell. We'd be skinned and eviscerated and be alive till the end.

The big red bug had his wings open but they were bent straight back. The bug was straining to take any of the weight. It was like trying to stop a cannonball with a handkerchief parachute.

And yet, and yet, were we slowing? No. But we were moving. Slight horizontal movement. Yes.

An inch. Another inch. The bug was taking some weight, trying to form enough of an airfoil to translate gravity's relentless drag into horizontal flight.

Glass rushing up.

Speeding down.

Reaching shards, some twenty feet long from base to serrated tip.

A slash. A cut. Blood gushing from my kneecap. I tried to strain back, tried to pull away, cleared my head, my shoulders, my calves, exposed everything else.

Inches. Horizontal movement, two descending arcs, the slope of daggers and the slight movement as the Red Wing took the weight.

Huge, jutting spear rushing up at me, it would open me up from crotch to breastbone, spill my guts like a fish, gut me, no way, strain back, screaming hoarse, muscles strained, miss!

And all at once we were zooming, zooming, still falling, but sweet heaven, zooming as much horizontal as vertical.

Spires of glass rose from that terrible valley floor, that hideous, impossible place, rose like fingers reaching to snatch us from the sky.

And now, now we slowed. And now, now we rose. We rose! Ganymede lifted me up, took me in his arms, pressed me to his hard chest, and I babbled a jerky, stuttering, "Thanks, man. I owe you. I owe you."

He nodded, solemn. "Exciting, wasn't it?"

So maybe he had a sense of humor after all.

We had killed all the Hetwan. Or rather, David had killed most of them with some assistance from the rest of us. Dionysus's illusions helped. And David withdrew his objection to letting the old fart have a drink. The god of parties wasn't worth much, but he was worth even less sober.

My big red bug came back, not at all apologetic. Wrapped me up in his tendrils again.

The Red Wings assembled and, hanging in midair above a plain I had come way too close to visiting, we decided we had no practical alternative but to go on. On to Ka Anor's city.

It was a long flight. Plenty of time to regret losing most of my toga. Plenty of time to regret plenty. Like the fact that April had fed a million dollars' worth of diamonds to some big alien insects. But mostly I regretted the fact that with each slow beat of the big red bugs' big red wings we were getting closer to the Hetwan headquarters.

It wasn't that Hetwan were hard to kill. They weren't. But there were way too many of them. Closer to the vast hypodermic mountain, Junkie Dream Mountain, I could see Hetwan everywhere, teeming up and down the slopes, clustered in their little half-adobe, half-wasp's-nest homes, filling the narrow streets.

It was impossible to guess numbers but I had the sense I was looking at a real city, not a village. A big city. Maybe not Chicago, but at least a Des Plaines or three. Way too many Ally McBugs.

How long till we reached the city? How long? Not long enough. My legs were numb from the tendrils cutting off the flow of blood. I leaned into the taut tendrils, wrapped my arms around them, and closed my eyes.

Impossible to sleep there. Impossible. But the city was still at least half an hour away, and I was so tired. Tired beyond the word *tired.* My body and mind needed to recharge for the next round of scared-as-hell.

Maybe the bug would drop me. Couldn't care about that. Too much, man. Too much.

"I call it the ZOG."

"What?" I blinked. CNN: Breaking News. My

brain was assaulted by images of falling, of a midair battle, of a terrible destination. My mind was already on overload. My boss, Mr. Trent, was laying all kinds of stuff off on me, and I was feeling edgy. Then, suddenly, wham-o, I learn that my other self, my Everworld self, was neck-deep in product.

"ZOG," one of my idiot coworkers said in a half whisper. His name was Randy, an older guy with a gut. He had a ponytail but looked as if he'd be bald before he hit thirty.

We were in my boss's office, a cramped cubbyhole off the supply room in the back of the copy shop. He had a small joint and had handed out cans of Busch to each of us. Us being me, Randy, and the scary little twerp named Keith.

I should have asked what ZOG was, they were all waiting expectantly, looking at me eagerly as though they'd all just said "knock, knock" and were waiting for me to move the joke along. But my real-world brain was focused on the now-old question of what exactly would happen to me if Everworld Christopher bit the dust.

Mr. Trent finally explained. "ZOG: Zionist Occupation Government. You see, our Constitution has been subverted, we've been sold out. This isn't a government of the white Christian people, and for the white Christian people, like it was intended to be. This is a government run by the Jews and the mud people."

I felt like my head was going to explode. It wasn't that I was surprised by Trent's opinions. Among the term papers and wills and sketches and divorce decrees I'd spent the last few days copying, there'd been a fair amount of weird political crap: rants and screeds off the Web, mostly. White this and white that.

So I knew Mr. Trent was into some strange stuff, but why drag me into it? I didn't have enough trouble? I was trying to sneak past Ka Anor. Starting a revolution was not the top thing on my priority list. Besides, like I was hot to join these losers? It was insulting. I wasn't Randy or Keith.

"A white Christian man can't make it in this world, not with the Jews and blacks and all the rest of 'em running everything." Mr. Trent gave me a shrewd look. "You know it, too, don't you?"

"Uh-huh," I said. Oh, man, what was I doing in this mess? I'd tried my best to avoid being dragged into these little after-work bitch sessions. I had a life, unlike these clowns.

Hell, I had two lives.

Any second now Everworld Christopher was going to snap awake out of his exhaustion nap.

Maybe already had. Maybe he/I was being burned or slashed or dropped. Maybe Ka Anor was finishing up eating one of my legs, smacking his lips, and saying, "Mmm, mmm, good."

"That's why the white man has to stick together. Loyalty. Like brothers."

"Okay." I nodded. "Well, thanks for the beer. I better get going."

Randy and Keith moved like they were going to stop me. I could take Keith down. No problem. Unless he was packing, which wouldn't surprise me.

But could I take all three? What was going on? Why was this happening? I couldn't be in the product in both universes at the same time, that was too much, that was way too much.

"I'm telling you all this for a reason," Mr. Trent said calmly.

I suppressed a groan. *Sit through it, Christopher. Listen to the little man talk, finish your beer, then book.* "Yeah?"

"Yeah," he mocked. "See, you have your head screwed on mostly right, Christopher. But you don't have the commitment. Now, that's what's important: commitment and loyalty."

I shot a look at Randy. At Keith. Keith had a tattoo of a death's-head with a swastika coming out of its mouth. The tattoo was on his chest. Like I said, a sick little perv, the kind of guy who grew up torturing bugs and family pets and now would like to graduate to bigger things.

And right then he looked like maybe he wanted me to be his Master's thesis.

CHAPTER XXI

"Well, you know, I'm not all that good in groups," I said lamely. "I'm not a joiner." I'd heard my mom use that phrase.

"You just want to be a slave? Or do you want to stand up to them, take this country back for the white Christian man? Are you scared, is that it?" Mr. Trent taunted. "Scared of the Hebrews?" He leaned close. He sniffed at me, as if he were a dog and I were a butt. "Or maybe that's some bad blood I smell."

I was more amazed than anything. How had I gotten myself into this? I was screwed in two universes at the same time. The very least was I'd lose my job, and as much of a nut as Mr. Trent was, he was easy to work for.

"Look, I respect all you're talking about and

all, but . . ." I looked from hard face to harder face to downright crazy face. "My mom is waiting for me. People are waiting for me, and they know where I am."

It sounded weak. It was weak.

"I guess I had you wrong, Hitchcock," Mr. Trent said coldly.

I sucked in a deep breath. The moment of menace was past. They would let me walk away. The reminder that people knew where I was and where to look for me had its effect.

I put down my empty beer can. "I'll see you guys tomorrow." We all knew that was b.s.

I turned, walked from the room, feeling prickly all up and down my back. I stepped outside into a cool fall night, took a deep, shaky breath, and jumped when I felt the touch on my shoulder.

Keith. He stood there, six inches shorter than me, a good seventy pounds lighter. He didn't have a shaved head or anything that would mark him as a skinhead. He wasn't wearing big army boots or leather or chains or anything. You couldn't see the tattoo unless he showed it to you. He had a pale wispy mustache and watery eyes.

"You know you ain't coming back, right?" he said.

"I kind of guessed that," I said.

"Don't need your kind. You're what we call a collaborator."

"Uh-huh."

He creeped me out. Creeped me out majorly, but I was on a public street, with a group of yapping college kids just across the street, and lights still on in the coffee shops and restaurants. So I wasn't scared in any immediate sense.

"What I come to tell you is, don't tell anyone what you seen or heard in there. You got that straight?"

"You little scrote, you think you scare me? I could drag your sorry little loser butt into that alley there and when I was done you'd spend a week in the hospital eating through a straw."

He smirked. "Yeah, you're a big guy. Real big. Not as big as my old man, who beat hell out of me every day since I was a little kid. You think you can threaten me? What I got to lose? Nothing. What do you got to lose? That's what you need to think about. You make any trouble for Mr. Trent, you need to think what you have to lose. Because whatever it is, whatever it is you care about, your mother, your girlfriend, if you have one, whatever it is, that's what I'll hurt."

I said a harsh pair of words, but they made no impact.

He said, "I'll hurt them bad. I know how, and I'll do it."

I walked home looking over my shoulder.

Now I had no job. And now I couldn't even go looking downtown anymore. I didn't want to run into Keith again. Not anytime soon.

My house looked good, all lit up. But when I got close enough I could hear the yelling. My mom and dad, about six glasses of wine and five martinis gone from the sound of it. They were yelling about this and that. Money, their sex lives, whether my dad was spending his lunch hours with "that Clorox blond." The usual.

I went around to the backyard, where we, like every family on the block, have a wooden swing set. I lay back on the cool yellow plastic slide. The acoustics were better back here. I couldn't hear specifics, just enough to know whether they were still winding up or winding down.

I wanted to go watch TV. That was all. Just watch some damned TV. I needed a laugh-track fix in the worst way.

"Life is sucking," I said to the stars.

And then I was flying, suspended beneath a big

red alien bug. I swear, for a few weird seconds, I was glad to be back.

"How do you sleep in the middle of this?" Jalil demanded angrily.

"Don't bust me, Jalil. I just lost my job."

"Yeah? How come?"

I laughed. "In a million years, you'd never guess."

XXII

And yet, despite another dose of my happy family, and despite the fact that I had managed to attract my own personal psycho who undoubtedly thought I was some NPR hippie liberal, I was not happy about what lay ahead.

Junkie Dream Mountain now filled my entire field of vision. It towered far above and extended far below. It went all the way from stage left to stage right.

Up close I saw even more of the detail: There were thousands of tiny windows and tiny doors, all glowing dully with gold or green lights. They gave the impression of being pinholes in one vast lantern. As if there was a humongous lightbulb down deep inside the mountain shining green-gold out through all these little windows.

"It's like a beehive," Jalil said. "Or a termite mound."

Probably true, but that wasn't all of it. The exterior of Junkie Dream was a real, functioning city, whatever else was down inside. I saw streets, crazy, jerky paths that wound up and down without making much sense. I saw what looked like stores or businesses, places anyway where seven or ten Hetwan would cluster and seem to be loading up on supplies. I saw nests of gut-bags, kind of all crammed together in a scooped-out bowl, fifteen or twenty of the ugly things, wings crunched, vibrating away like they might all erupt at any moment.

It was a vertical city. Homes, if that's what they were, piled one atop the next, with tiny-stepped ladders or shallow stairs leading up and down. It would go perfectly vertical for a while, then step back to make way for a street, then go vertical again.

"Why the steps?" Jalil wondered aloud. "They can fly. But they have walkways and steps and ladders and they're obviously using them."

"Not just them," David pointed out. "Look, there's some humans."

I spotted a group of maybe a dozen humans, loaded down with big burlap bags. Relief. Humans. Humans were good.

Or not. Keith. He wouldn't really go after my family, would he? My mom? My little brother? Sick piece of crap. Weird feeling, as if I should be there to take care of things. I mean, I was there. I was here and there. And still I felt like I should be back there.

The real world was supposed to be a break from all this, some downtime, some safe time. It was Mr. Trent's fault. Was there some reason Hitler's Mini-Me had to try and drag me into his psychodrama?

"Here's an idea, Christopher," I said to myself. "How about focusing on one mess at a time?"

"What?" April asked.

She was near. Closer than I'd realized. In fact, the Red Wings were bunching together.

"Nothing," I said to April.

"I think we're getting ready to land," she said.

"Yeah. Who knew I'd come to like hanging from a flying bug?"

"Beats the alternative."

We were slowly settling toward a platform that was the mirror image of the place where we'd picked up the bugs. Coming in for a landing.

Ganymede said, "They will set us down yonder."

We weren't the only bug-riders coming in for a landing. Just ahead of us were three dwarfs. With them were seven Red Wings carrying crates.

"Hell of a way to do business," I said. "I hope the Hetwan pay well."

"Can't the Red Wings just keep flying?" David asked Dionysus. "They could fly us straight on around, to the far side of the crater."

Dionysus naturally had no idea, though he did stop swigging wine long enough to consider the possibility.

David tried it out. He yelled up to his Red Wing, "Take us away from the city, to the far side of the crater."

No answer. No answer and no reaction. We stayed on our glide path. And five minutes later the Red Wings released us on the platform, halfway up the side of the world's biggest termite mound.

The big red bugs then scooted off to sit passively, wings folded, tentacles coiled, awaiting their next fare like taciturn taxi drivers.

We huddled together, the six of us. It was breezy and hot and somehow, here in the home office of nasty, the sun no longer shined. There was a haze or a gloom or maybe just a really bad mood that hung in the air.

Shallow stairs led off the platform. The dwarfs were counting their crates and calling in their deep, strained voices to a dark cave that opened onto the platform.

From this cave emerged creatures that seemed startlingly familiar.

"Beetles," April said.

Not the bug. The car. Three bright yellow things like half-sized Volkswagen Beetles came rolling out. They were clearly alive. They were clearly odd. Where the four wheels should be they had four things that at first glance could have been dark brown tires.

But these tires didn't turn so much as pulsate or stretch or . . . something. Imagine a big balloon tire. Imagine three bowling balls trapped inside. Imagine the bowling balls rolling inside the tire, each one stretching the spongy rubber and moving the "car" forward by six or eight inches. Then another bowling ball would slide down to make contact with the road and sort of squeeze the bug forward another few inches. But all this happened on all four "wheels" with enough speed that the creature, the VW, actually moved at a perky walking speed.

The dwarfs loaded their stuff onto the VW's, and off they went. The VW's didn't care if it was flat ground or stairs or steep, narrow pathway. Up and off they went with the dwarfs keeping pace.

"Let's follow them," David said.

"Indeed," Dionysus agreed. "And let us summon forth these bearer creatures to carry us."

"Let's not," David said. "Let's walk."

Dionysus frowned. "I am a god. You, a mere mortal. You must defer, my good fellow. You must learn your place if you are to be among the gods of Olympus."

"Uh-huh. Here's the thing: I have a sword. You have a glass of burgundy. And let me point something else out to you: Those VW's are hanging onto their crates. They have them locked in with suction or something. Me, I want to be able to run."

"Mmm," Dionysus said. "You make a good point. And would anyone like a drink?"

Chapter XXIII

I ascended the steps, up off the platform, away from the Red Wings for whom I'd begun to have some affection. They had carried me over the valley of the shadow of death, and while I'd feared some evil, they'd carried my sad self for a long way.

"I feel like we should tip them," I said.

"I guess we walk around this mountain," David said doubtfully. "Get to the other side, see if they have some Red Wings over there who can carry us on to the far side of the crater."

"It is much shorter to travel through the center of the city," Ganymede pointed out.

"Yeah. Maybe so. But that's where Ka Anor is, right?"

"Yes. Ka Anor is within the mountain," Ganymede confirmed.

"Let's go the long way," April said. She held out her hand, ushering Ganymede to a place ahead of her in the line.

"You are pathetic," I whispered to her. "You know, he's not a piece of meat. The boy saved my life."

"Hard to handle that, huh?"

"We're always about six inches away from dead around here, W.T.E. I'll pay him back, sooner or later, you know it, and we'll be cool."

In a louder voice April said, "Shouldn't we have a story ready in case someone asks? I mean, why are we here?"

That made David flush, the way he does when he's made a mistake. "Yeah. Yeah, we need a story. April's right."

"The usual?" Jalil suggested.

"Why not?" David agreed, still biting his lip at having failed to anticipate. The guy was going to have a nervous breakdown before he was old enough to rent a car. Way too wound up.

"The usual" was our story that we were minstrels. It had worked with the Vikings. Hadn't worked at all with the Aztecs. But the flea-bitten mutants of the deep woods had bought it. Would the Hetwan?

I sang, "And you tell me, over and over and

over again, my fray-und, that you don't believe we're on the eve of destruction."

"Very funny," Jalil said disapprovingly. But then he laughed a sardonic laugh.

"I'm going down, I'm going down, down, down, down dow-own," I sang.

"Christopher, you're like the encyclopedia of old stuff. TV, music . . ." April paused for a well-timed beat. "Attitudes."

"Jeff Beck isn't old. It's classic," I said. "Just like me. Oh, man. Look at that."

We had not gone far. We'd made it up over a rise, half crab-walking to cling to the badly made pathways. We'd reached an intersection of paths where Hetwan scuttled by going one way and a fairy couple flitted by in the other direction.

What caught my eye was a pole mounted in the middle of the intersection. It wasn't big, just a stick. But atop the stick was a sort of wad that might have been the lifetime accumulated chew of a Denny's waitress. It was stuck on the pole, kind of gray-pink. The sides had been crudely smoothed, and on each smooth side was a picture. It looked like one of those old computer pictures made with lots of little x's and o's. Like it had all been done with stabs of a ballpoint pen, hundreds of dots.

You had to look at the picture for a while to make sense of it. The senses of the artist were alien, after all. The perspective lacked any kind of real familiarity with the subject. Like it had been drawn from third-hand descriptions.

And yet, for all that, there was no doubt who it was. I felt like someone had dragged a sharp icicle up my spine.

"Senna," April hissed.

Senna Wales's likeness stared out from all four sides of the gum wad.

"A Hetwan wanted poster," Jalil said.

David nodded, wordless. Poor dumb sap, even here, even now, staring at pinpricks on an alien spitwad, he was drawn, trapped, touched, moved.

"They're looking for her," Jalil said. "They're making sure everyone who passes through this city understands that Ka Anor is looking for her."

"Do you know this person?" Ganymede asked.

"Is she really as cold and passionless as this makes her seem?" Dionysus asked, concerned, I guess, at being confronted with an entirely different sort of human woman.

I said, "You won't be wanting to invite her to any of your parties. She's not fun. Very Goth, you know."

"She's a *witch*," Jalil said, like the word tasted

bad. "She's the gateway. Supposedly. Loki wants her. Ka Anor wants her."

"A witch? Hmmm." Dionysus considered that. You could see the wheels turning in the old lecher's mind. I guarantee you he was picturing her dressed in some skimpy Greek version of a witch costume, serving eye-of-newt hors d'oeuvres at his next hoedown.

"At least it isn't our pictures," April said. She showed no sympathy for her half sister. Not a close family.

"And too soon for Dionysus or Ganymede to be posted," Jalil said. "But so much for the theory that Hetwan wouldn't recognize a specific face."

We moved on, past the poster, but Senna hung over us, preying on our minds, quieting our lame attempts at whistling-past-the-graveyard conversation. I could almost see the energy draining out of David.

We moved on, not wanting to appear too interested in the poster of Senna. There were Hetwan everywhere. On the paths, on the steps, within open windows.

Complex relationships. Each of us and Senna. I knew my problem with her. I knew David's problem with her. April and Jalil, and why they so loathed her, all that was a mystery.

We were preoccupied, the four of us, so at first we didn't even notice how Dionysus managed to screw us.

He was at the back, out of sight. A mistake. And when I thought to turn around and check on him, it was too late.

He was now accompanied by a shapely green nymph and a woman who bore a weird resemblance to what's her name, the *Sabrina* chick in one of her sexy, non-Sabrina moments. Walking just behind Dionysus was a strapping lad carrying a barrel of Chianti.

Dionysus had decided to throw a party. He'd summoned a good time out of thin air. Made things appear where they couldn't.

And even the Hetwan knew what that meant.

A Hetwan screech.

Ahead on the path, to the left, to the right, above us on different trails, from the open, light-filled windows and doors, Hetwan heads turned. Turned, stared, focused, fixed.

On us.

Helpless. What were we going to do? We were black ants on the red ants' mound. They were everywhere. And we with nowhere to run.

"In!" David snapped.

The Hetwan rushed. From everywhere. Down, up, all sides at once. They'd spotted a god, and Ka Anor was looking for a snack.

David stopped beside one of the many windows. A Hetwan inside was rushing to emerge. David skewered him.

"Move!" he yelled.

He grabbed April and practically threw her inside. Dionysus was crowding to be next, bleating fearfully, babbling about his "possible error, but all for the best of reasons."

It was panic. Dionysus hung on the windowsill, Jalil pushed him hard. In went the god of the party, in went Jalil, I was grabbing the window sides, hauling myself in. The Hetwan wave crashed around us. David slashed. I fell in through the window. Reached a hand for David. Grabbed his free hand, yanked him back, hauled hard, got him to tumble back toward us, with fiery Hetwan spitwads everywhere.

A small room. Open at one end. A darkened tunnel. Leading inward, oh, God, not the place I wanted to go, not into this place. I looked back, like maybe somehow I could jump back out through the window and live.

Ganymede!

He was still out there. The Hetwan all over him, a dozen alien hands grabbing, tearing, beating him down by sheer weight.

"Come on!" David yelled in my ear.

I froze. Stared. Had to go get him. Had to save him.

"Dammit, let's go," David said. "We can't save him. We can't save ourselves."

I broke free, tore my eyes away. My insides twisted. He'd saved my life, not an hour before. He'd come within inches of splattering himself all over the broken-glass valley to save me.

I ran. Ran and wanted to live and didn't deserve to. Shame on me. Shame was on me, in me, but I ran.

Out of the bare cubbyhole of a room. Down darkened tubes. Hetwan! A rush of them from a side tunnel.

David slashed.

I slammed into them bodily. Reckless. I smashed them back, a fullback hitting the sidelines and scattering the waterboys and hangers-on.

Back to running. Hetwan on our heels. More ahead. Trapped.

"Keep moving," David yelled.

We hit them, a mass of us, solid-bodied, heavy-boned humans and pseudohumans hitting creatures that were light enough to fly. Mammals versus birds. That's what it was like. We slammed them, stomped over them, heard them crunch brittlely under our weight. The Hetwan weren't armed, not yet.

Running, feet plodding on spongy floor. Like the place were carved out of dough.

The Hetwan couldn't use their wings in the

tubes. And on foot we were faster. Easy win for us. Except for the fact that we were outnumbered about ten thousand to one.

The tube went down, steep as a middle-of-the-ride roller-coaster drop. Jalil tripped. The rest of us plowed into and over him. Then it was a free fall, a rolling, mad jumble of arms and legs, shouts and cries, grunts of pain, sharp exhalations as flying feet caught chests, elbows whacked noses.

We rolled, then straightened out enough to slide. Yee-haw, a dry water slide, down, down, twisting this way and that, but always down.

I was on my back. Looked back, saw Hetwan zooming headfirst after us. The Hetwan slid faster. Less resistance, even though they were lighter.

I was picking up speed. Dionysus's bald head was just inches from my feet. The nearest Hetwan was gaining, aiming for me, aiming his Super-Soaker. Gaining. He would burn holes in my scalp, burn through my skull, set my brain on fire.

I lifted my hands over my head, arms straight up, elbows slightly bent, fists clenched. Would the SuperSoaker drill into me? Better than being burned alive.

I jammed the sides of my shoes into the tube walls, slowed, the Hetwan rushed, suddenly too fast. My fists caught his shoulders. His needle point scraped the side of my head, stopped just short of cutting into my own shoulders.

The Hetwan spread his wings just a little to brake, slow his speed.

I kept up the braking pressure, shifted my grip to a hold on his head. I dug my fingers in tight, released my "brakes," tucked my legs to lower resistance, and sped away.

I accelerated just as the Hetwan was braking. His head came away in my hands. The body left behind jerked spasmodically, wings jerked open, tiny bones and exoskeleton jabbed, grabbed, caught, crumpled. The Hetwan's body slowed, spun, was slammed by descending Hetwan. A pileup on the interstate.

I held the Hetwan's head, SuperSoaker still in place. The head was almost as big as my own, the eyes huge, fly eyes, glittering multifaceted.

I wanted to throw it away, but it would roll after me. Had to hold on. Had to keep my grip on the foul thing. Still-moving mouth parts tickled my bare stomach.

Suddenly, we were out of the tube, rolling across an open floor. Stop. Pain. Gasp for air. Look around. The five of us, the five minus Ganymede, the five who still had some faint chance at life gasped and panted and moaned over bruises.

"What is that?" Jalil asked, staring at the Hetwan head.

"Getting ready for Halloween, man."

"Where's Ganymede?" April asked.

No answer. What answer could I give? No forgiveness for losing him. No forgiveness for cowardice.

A broken, twisted, headless Hetwan rolled from the tube. Other Hetwan pushed past him, tried to stand.

I pointed the Hetwan head at them. I wrapped one arm under the SuperSoaker, and with the other fist I punched the back of the head.

A lava spitwad flew from the head. A miss. I yelped in surprise. I took aim this time and punched again. The spitwad flew. It hit one of the advancing Hetwan in his chest.

The Hetwan screeched. The fire burned a neat round hole in his hard plastic shell.

I aimed again, punched. Caught the same Hetwan a second time, in the face.

"Let's go!" David yelled.

I went. We all went. Ganymede too far away now to think about. We'd slid forever. Where were we?

Running across a stale dough floor. Darkness above suggested an endless void. I had the creepy feeling that we were inside a living thing. The creepy sensation that the spongy floor felt the passage of our feet.

Chapter XXV

We ran through the living tunnels, the dark veins and arteries of the vast hive. Ran and ran, slower, slower, dragging Dionysus along, stopping, gasping, panting, hands on knees, bent over, barely able to stand.

We'd been burned. Beaten. Scared. Exhausted. Shamed.

Where were the Hetwan? How could they have lost us? This was their home, their turf. Impossible that they could have lost us.

And yet, we were alone. Alone, the four of us and the useless immortal. Alone in near pitch-darkness. Alone with the sense that we were watched, seen, followed at a distance.

Were the Hetwan scared at last? Had they realized that they were no match for us in battle? If so, then they were fools. One concerted rush and they would have us.

"What's going on?" Jalil wondered.

David shook his head. Sweat dripped from his downturned face. April's breathing had a pained sound to it. Like she was breathing smoke.

Dionysus was the only one of us not tired, not really. He was slow, he complained, he bitched, I hated his guts, the huge pain in the ass, but he was recovered fully. Immortal. Weariness was an act with him. All humanity, all human weakness was an act. Even his drunkenness, I suspected. He'd lived. Ganymede was taken.

I wanted to pull my hair out by the roots. I wanted to gouge my own eyes out. No forgiveness for this. Ganymede had saved me. I'd failed him. No forgiveness for that. No forgiveness.

"Better keep moving. Although I'll be damned if I have a clue what direction," David admitted. He looked at a burn on his arm.

I felt my own burns. My own bruises and scrapes and aches and torn muscles. But all that was nothing. All that was welcome.

No forgiveness. How do you not risk death to save the one who saved you? How do you not die trying? How do you still think of yourself as a man?

I was a useless piece of crap of a human being. Losers like Trent and Keith thought I belonged with them, and Jesus, maybe they were right. Maybe they'd seen in me what I didn't want to see in myself.

I felt Ganymede's hand as he'd taken my weight, taken my weight as I screamed and cried and begged indifferent heaven for salvation. He'd have died, immortal or not, he'd have been ripped to shreds, he'd have died if we'd hit. And I had run.

"Christopher, wake up, man." It was David. The others were already moving. Already staggering, walking, dragging their sorry selves down the corridors.

"Come on, man. Dionysus says he knows the direction."

"Screw him."

David grabbed my upper arm, yanked me along. Dragged me till I would walk.

"Maybe he got away," David said. Like he'd been reading my thoughts. "You don't know. Maybe he got away. I mean, we did, right?"

I didn't say anything. I couldn't grab onto that hope. But I could let it live. I could hold open that possibility, however slight. Maybe. Maybe the big fag made it. Yeah, maybe.

Dionysus led the way, not exactly mourning

the loss of his companion in partying. He led the way, chattering about his infallible sense of where Olympus lay, in what direction, no matter how far, no matter darkness or light.

He led the way and the floor beneath our feet watched us.

"It grows light up ahead," Dionysus said.

It did grow light. A greenish light. Not the sun, not even the Everworld sun. And there was a noise, a sound, vast, endless, repetitive.

"That's some kind of chant," April said. "It's weird. Strange key. The scale is wrong. But listen, it sounds almost religious."

We crept forward, little by little, slow, slow, David out front with Galahad's sword drawn. Jalil drew his little knife and opened the blade. I had dropped my own macabre weapon. I had nothing but my battered fists, and would I even use them?

The tunnel ended. We stood at the edge. We looked out into a space so vast it could have been used to park the entire fleet of Goodyear blimps and still have room left over for the Blue Angels to do flybys.

It was cylindrical in shape. A honeycombed curve of wall. Thousands, tens of thousands of open holes, tunnels like our own. We were maybe a third of the way up. High overhead I looked at night sky. The open hypodermic hole of Junkie Dream Mountain.

Hetwan by the thousands glided down from the holes, down to join a dense mass of the insects all clustered below. So many I couldn't see an inch of vacant floor.

They were chanting. A rhythmic sound, not quite musical, but hypnotic. Sexual. A sound that in its vastness, in its relentlessness, its insinuating seductiveness reached down into my brain and made me want to join in, made me want to be a part of it.

But the Hetwan were merely the congregation. Their one god was the center of it all: Ka Anor.

He was vast. But he was no one thing. Ka Anor was everything. Every nightmare, every terror, every image from every horror movie.

He was a different thing, a different face every time you blinked your eyes. A seething, towering mass of liquid filth. A screaming jaw filled with teeth like blood-soaked stalactites. A huge, exaggerated Hetwan with a hundred eyes. An erupting volcano dribbling out burning corpses.

Impossible. He could not be a hundred different things. It was in my head. It was all in my imagination. I knew that. But the animal moan that rose from my throat was evidence of a deeper truth: Ka Anor was fear.

Then came the Red Wing, circling down from high above. And in his tentacles, hanging there, helpless, the young man whose beauty had drawn Zeus's roving, randy eye to the fields of Troy.

CHAPTER XXVI

"No," I whispered.

The Red Wing flew, inexorable. The chanting became more emotional, more fervent. The Hetwan were anticipating. They were excited.

Ganymede struggled, but no good.

Ka Anor formed into a huge, fluid beast, all head and shoulders and reaching claws.

From the mouth, a tongue. A tongue that was a cloud of tiny insects, a billion spiders, a billion maggots, all the army ants in the world, all formed into a lascivious tongue that buzzed and seethed and curled up toward the doomed immortal.

"NO!" I screamed.

The sound was lost in the chant. David grabbed me from behind, clamped his hand over my mouth. I fought. Crazed. Out of control. I bit and clawed.

Jalil pinned my arms and held on tight. And David kept saying, "Not your fault, man, not your fault."

Ka Anor's tongue wrapped around the small figure of Ganymede. The billions of insects, those billions of tiny ripping, tearing teeth, the living filth conjured up by the god-eater, began to strip Ganymede of flesh.

I screamed.

April put her hand over my eyes and prayed to Mary to intercede, to keep this evil from us. Hail Mary. Hail Mary.

No one covered my ears. Ganymede screamed for a long time. The chanting became frantic. Ecstatic. The Hetwan were witnessing a sacrament.

It seemed to last forever. But finally Ganymede was quiet. And the Hetwan chant was stilled. And when David and Jalil and April released me, I was quiet, too.

The Hetwan were asleep, or groggy at least. They slept the sleep of the righteous, having served Ka Anor and witnessed his satisfaction.

Ka Anor was nothing now. An empty space at the center of the hive. Had he ever been real? Was he just some nightmare conjured up out of the needs of the Hetwan?

Real enough.

It took us hours to work our way around the core. Hours of expecting the Hetwan to arise and drag Dionysus from us, maybe kill us quickly, if we were lucky.

Dionysus was still Dionysus. I guess gods don't change much. I guess they are what they are, embodying the virtues and weaknesses they represent. Life was still a party for Dionysus. Always would be. Till he was at last fed to Ka Anor.

We found Red Wings on the far side of Junkie Dream Mountain. Passed more wanted posters for Senna. The Hetwan were just beginning to make their way back onto the pathways of their world, bleary as drunks after a binge.

None of us said much. Just the perfunctory words necessary to finding our way. We reached a platform of Red Wings and took off.

It would be a long trip to the far side. A long flight and I was so tired. So sick-tired.

I slept.

I was walking along our street. Carrying what? Chinese food. Yeah, I'd gone a few blocks down to the restaurant for some moo goo and some kung pao and some fried rice.

I got the CNN: Breaking News. The bag

dropped. Rice burst onto the sidewalk. I knelt down, stupidly tried to shovel the rice back into the container.

I was a coward. Ganymede had saved me. I'd let him die. I'd let him die.

"Wasn't your fault," I told myself. "Wasn't your fault," I echoed David's words.

No forgiveness for this. No forgiveness.

My insides had spilled out onto the sidewalk with the Chinese food. I was hollowed out. Empty. What was I? What was Christopher Hitchcock?

Nothing. Fear and hatred and lust and jealousy. What was I, to live?

The trees were in full, brilliant fall mode. Golden leaves and green, here and there a first, early gush of red. The air was clear and cool. The street was lined with the Victorian homes of the smug and prosperous. Two-car garages held a standard-issue minivan beside the Mercedes, the Audi, the BMW.

I walked in a dream. Memories that shouldn't be mine. A failure, a betrayal that shouldn't be mine, but was.

I reached my house, clutching a torn and greasy paper bag. My little brother's bike was on the porch. Strange. Like it had been carefully placed so as to block the door. It was standing sideways, centered.

I went up the front stairs. The plastic of the bike seat was torn. No, cut. Cut in the shape of a swastika.

And beneath the swastika, a small letter *K*.

I started drinking then and there in the real world, and continued when I crossed back over. It seemed kind of funny, you know. The first-ever two-universe binge. Both of me were drinking. It was easier in Everworld, of course, with Dionysus always ready to pour.

David gave me some grief, but then he let it go. It didn't matter. The Hetwan didn't come after us. They never figured out we had two gods with us, not just one. And if we were leaving, hey, that was fine by them.

On the far side of that hellish crater we happened upon a troupe of dwarf traders on their way to Ka Anor. They had ponies loaded down with stuff. April convinced them to sell the ponies to us, handing over the last of the diamonds.

Thus ended our brief period of wealth.

But the ponies meant we could travel faster. And doze more often. You wouldn't think it would be possible to sleep while jouncing along beneath yammering trees on the back of a pony. But you'd be wrong. A quart of Dionysus's best will let you sleep anywhere.

A couple of days later we were out of Hetwan country, traveling beneath a bread-baking sun. So hot the booze went straight from throat to sweat glands. I was in a fog. A bi-universal fog of self-pity. And I'll tell you something about self-pity: being drunk doesn't lessen it any. No, booze will take the edge off guilt, take the sting out of shame. But it waters the self-pity, grows it nice and strong.

Here in this uncomfortably hot country Dionysus was in his element. The four of us were now nothing but weary, weirdly-clothed clowns in the company of the great Dionysus. We passed through clean, colorful towns and were met with flower bouquets and everyone's unmarried daughters. These were the D-man's people, and he was going to show them a good time. The vino flowed from the god to the people, from the people to the god, and a good bit of it flowed through me.

By the weird geography of Everworld we had crossed from an alien landscape into ancient Greece. The houses, when I bothered to raise my blurred vision for a look, were like a Santa Fe thing, all smooth edges and thick walls. Very Southwest. Only instead of the whitewash you always see in travel posters of the Greek Islands, these were painted blue and pink and green and gold.

Nice country. Too damned hot, but the people looked okay, and they were friendly.

"Dionysus, man. I'm dry over here."

My cup refilled, although I was getting the sense that Dionysus was sick of me. Fair enough, I was sick of me, too.

And then, maybe, I don't know, three days, five days, whatever, after . . . After Ka Anor, Dionysus at last said, "Olympus!"

He said it with a flourish. "Olympus!"

And you know, it would have been very impressive, very Hollywood, but for the fact that the sky five miles to our north, to the far side of Olympus, was dark with Hetwan.

Chapter XXVII

I took a deep breath and looked up at Olympus. It was something, all right. A mountain. Not exactly one of the Rockies, but I guess it was a mountain.

Olympus. I was going to be immortal. Of course, immortal only held as long as you didn't smash yourself at nine hundred miles an hour into glass spears. Or get eaten alive by some alien nightmare.

David rode beside me. "We're about to enter Olympus. Maybe it's time for you to snap out of it."

I turned a wobbly glare on him. "Snap out of it? Why? Want to make a good impression on those guys up there?"

"Yeah," he said. "I do. Dionysus promised you immortality, you know."

"Cool," I drawled. "I can be me forever."

"Okay, look, Christopher, that's enough of this." He took my pony's reins and made me stop. We were in a vineyard. Or at least there were grapevines on either side of us. Dionysus was up ahead, surrounded by half-dressed babes, some probably real, some false. What did it matter?

"I don't get this, Christopher. I really don't. I'm as sorry as you are about Ganymede. No one deserves that. But we've seen some sick stuff here. That was sick, that was sad, but jeez, Christopher, is it really worse than what Hel has going on? Or what Huitzilopoctli does? Look, that's Olympus up there. No human sacrifice. No burying people alive. No alien gods chewing up big gods. None of that —"

I swung, hit him in the side of the head, fell into him, carried him over and both of us fell to the ground in a heap.

"Get the hell off —" he yelled, but I grabbed him, bear-hugged him, held him down then started punching him, everything I had.

I'm bigger than David. If I'd been sober he'd have been in trouble. But I was in the bag, no thought, nothing but hatred and rage and uncontrolled violence.

David got a knee up and kicked me in the

groin. I rolled off, face in the dirt, weeping and holding myself.

David stood up, brushed himself off, and glared down at me. "Dammit, Christopher, what the hell is your malfunction?"

The others, April and Jalil, reined in, watching, amazed I suppose.

"No malfunction here," I grated into the dirt. "I'm fine. Here I am. Fine. Alive. No one chewed the skin off me. You know why? You know why I'm fine? Because I'm not splattered all over, that's why. And there's some little psycho checking out my family, but see, I'm fine, won't be me that gets hurt."

David looked at Jalil. "You know what this is?"

Jalil shrugged. He was watching me. Me the virus, him the scientist on the other end of the microscope. I was interesting to him. Jalil said, "I guess he's feeling guilty over Ganymede. Thinks he should have saved him."

"Wow, Jalil, you are a genius," I said savagely. "Wow, turns out you are smart after all."

"What happens here isn't your fault, dude," David said. "We're neck deep in a sewer. We're all going to end up stinking. I was there. I told you then to let him go. We couldn't save him."

I got up slowly. My brain was sobered up, but

my body was dehydrated and poisoned. I brushed off the few rags I'd picked up from the dwarfs. "Maybe I could have saved him. Maybe not. But see, the bitch is, for that split second, when the Hetwan came down around him, that split second, I thought, *screw him.* See, that's the thing. You know what else, David, my hero David? So did you."

David's jaw clenched. He said nothing.

April looked sharply at David and whispered, "Oh, no," like she was witnessing a tragedy and couldn't do anything to stop it.

"And we both know, David, we both know why we could let him die and think 'screw him.' All right? We know, you and me. We're the same on that. Only, he saved my life. And when he did, I said, 'I owe you one.' Something to say, what else are you going to say? But it was true, too. I owed him my . . ."

I couldn't talk. Sucked air through a clenched throat. "I owed him. My life. One life. Screw him. See?"

I was babbling. Not making any sense. Making an ass of myself. Being a fool.

"You have to let it go," Jalil said. "No sense in torturing yourself over the past."

"He wants to be forgiven," April said.

Words.

I mounted my pony and together we headed toward Olympus.

A few hours later I was sober. Sick, wanting to die, stomach shredded, head exploding, but sober. I was sober and sick and I was on Olympus, home of the gods.

How can I describe that place? I saw a movie once, forget what it's called. Had that guy who used to be on *L.A. Law.* Anyway, they had Olympus. It was like some Greek temple and some clouds.

The real gods of Olympus did a little better for themselves than that.

The top of the mountain was razed flat, forming a mesa, I guess you'd call it. Flat as a table. But the ground was a floor, and that floor was huge squares of marble caulked with gold. Marble and gold. And where the marble would end the half-acre mosaic would begin. Here there were millions of perfectly-joined one-inch tiles of silver, of ebony, of sapphire, of emerald, of gold, all formed into huge scenes of gods at play, chasing nymphs, riding winged horses, kicking ass on other gods.

There was a sort of main drag, a street as wide as a six-lane interstate including divider, lined with columned marble mansions on either side. These were the buildings the old Greeks, all those

Athenians and Spartans or whatever had in mind when they built temples. These were what they wished they could make, but it was as if those humans were stuck working with Lego's and Lincoln Logs. The gods built with marble and diamond, and gold, gold, gold.

Here and there, groups of them walked by. Immortals. Gods. Nymphs and satyrs and all the usual immortal riffraff, but also big, powerful males and terrifying females, all brimming with power and confidence and easy swagger. Either they didn't realize the Hetwan were massing to the north of their happy home, or else, being gods and all, they figured they'd handle it.

They sure didn't look at us like we were the last troops coming to enlist at the Alamo.

We were bums. We were derelicts. We were filthy, squalid, shabby creatures on tired, dirty horses. The immortals waved or called to Dionysus, and laughed at the sight of us.

At the far end of the street, past fountains that jetted oceans' worth of clear water from diamond nymphs and golden horses' heads, past rows of statues, past silver trees and patches of impossibly bright flowers, stood one mansion, one temple big enough to hold all the others.

"The home of my father, Great Zeus," Dionysus said grandly, waving his chubby fingers.

"Wait till he sees that I have returned. You've never seen a revel, my mortal friend. Never anything to equal what we'll throw. And of course, I shall tell him of your service. He is sure to offer you immortality and a home here, among us."

"I'd be happy with some clean clothes and a shower," Jalil said.

Dionysus put his arm around me. I guess we were compadres now. Me and him, the only drunks.

"Immortality," he said. "You'll enjoy it. Mortals who ascend to these heights are rare, very rare."

"Like Ganymede," I said.

"Yes," Dionysus said brightly. Then, as an afterthought added, "Poor boy. A pity. He was very popular. Anyway, we shall throw a party in your honor as the newest of the immortals of Olympus."

I didn't say anything. The crazy old lecher Dionysus had shown me a way out. Shown me a path to find some peace.

I owed Ganymede a life. Sooner or later, this universe or my own, one of them was going to kill me. But that wouldn't settle my debt. Everyone dies.

Not everyone gives up immortality.

I closed my eyes and saw myself falling, falling

forever toward that shattered glass plain. Saw a hand reach for me. Felt my weight being taken.

I felt it again, now. Felt a lightness I hadn't felt since that day. It wasn't enough. I wasn't rewriting the past. Wasn't making good on what I'd screwed up. But I was paying what I could pay for now.

Maybe the day would come when I could mess up Ka Anor. Maybe he'd come here. Maybe by then I'd have the stick big enough to beat that evil thing till he couldn't get up again.

Maybe then I'd be even.

I laughed, which made David look at me in surprise.

"What's funny?"

"Me. Some folks find religion. Some folks join A.A. Me? I meet a big gay Trojan. Go figure that out."

"Uh-huh," David said warily.

I looked around, saw a seven-foot-tall Jennifer Lopez in an easy-remove toga give me the eye. Must have been the diaper look I had going on.

Olympus, huh? Cool.

EVER WORLD #VII GATEWAY TO THE GODS

Suddenly the door flew open. David's sword was half-drawn before we had a chance to see that it was a woman. Youngish, maybe thirty. Dark hair and dark eyes and both wild-looking.

She stood still, rolled her eyes upward, like she was having a seizure and in a low moan intoned:

"Olympus by the Hetwan hordes besieged,
Hellas' gods Ka Anor shall feed,
'Less strangers bring the Witch to heed,
The alien blacksmiths' secret need."

Having delivered that imperfect rhyme, she fluttered her eyes, then stared at us like we were the ones who had burst into her room.

"Who are you?" David demanded.

"I am Cassandra," the woman said.

"Oh, please," Jalil said. "Cassandra was the prophet, the oracle. Yeah, Cassandra was the oracle who always spoke the truth but was cursed never to be believed."

"Yes," the woman said with petulant resignation replacing the wild-child look. "I know."

"So, wait," David said, frowning. "So she always speaks the truth, but no one believes her? So . . . So we should believe her. Right?"

"Do you believe her?" I asked.

David shook his head. "No."